This is a work of fiction. The events in this novel are imaginary.
Copyright © 2019 Richelle Atkin

All rights reserved. No part of this publication may be reproduced, distributed, or transmitted in any form or by any means, including photocopying, recording, or other electronic or mechanical methods, without the prior written permission of the publisher, except in the case of brief quotations embodied in critical reviews and certain other noncommercial uses permitted by copyright law. For permission requests, write to Richelle at info@richelleatkin.com.

CHAPTER 1:
Hello! And Welcome!

Tightening of the chest, shooting pain down the left arm, shooting pain up the neck, shortness of breath, cold sweat, nausea. They say these are the warning signs of a heart attack. But Alice had none of them. She was alive, and then she was dead. It was as simple as that.

***

Mac stood in the small bathroom located just off the kitchen. His hands gripped either side of the porcelain sink and he stared down. It had happened earlier than he expected and he was nervous. He looked at his feet and saw Roo patiently sitting and staring back up at him. Mac smiled and scratched behind his pal's ear before straightening his powder blue ruffled tux one last time and looking up at himself in the mirror. There was no reflection, but it was a force of habit that even fifty-some years hadn't broken. And it didn't matter either; he knew exactly what he looked like: 17, blond comb over, baby blues and pearly whites. He was the classic mid-century, all-American prom date.

"Alright Daddy-O" he turned back to Roo. "Showtime."

The large, curved staircase leading to the upstairs bedrooms was creaky and required Mac to take slow, gentle steps. Roo trailed quietly behind, perfectly matching his pace. Mac knew what Alice was going though and didn't want to frighten her any more than he already knew he would. He had only done this one other time and it hadn't gone exactly to plan. This time, however, he was hoping for a smooth run.

The bedroom door was already half open as Mac walked up to it. When the time was right, he only had to give it one small push for it to fully open. Since they had been living in the same house for almost six months, Mac had of course seen Alice before, but that night would be the first time that she would see him. And everyone else for that matter.

Mac peeked around the corner of the door and watched, picking his moment. He had learned that timing really was everything with this sort of thing. Looking at Alice then, Mac noticed that there was something sharper, clearer, and more concrete about her, which he found amusing, given the circumstances. He leaned against the doorframe with Roo sitting at his feet and watched her for a moment as she stood staring at the bed. He could tell she hadn't figured it out yet. Instead, her gaze kept shifting from her husband's sleeping body over to what looked like her own sleeping body.

Middle Ground

As Alice processed, Mac noted the red and white plaid flannel pajamas she was wearing and thought it unfortunate attire to have died in. Then again, he thought, looking down at himself, given the opportunity, perhaps he would have selected something different, too.

"Time to introduce ourselves." he whispered to Roo before pushing the master bedroom door wide open. "Hello! And welcome!" Mac said, holding out his arms with the enthusiasm of a circus ringmaster.

At his voice Alice immediately spun and shuffled backwards until the backs of her knees knocked against the edge of the bed. She tumbled onto the mattress but quickly jumped up when she realized she had landed on her own body.

"Get out! Get out of my house!" Alice yelled, holding her fists up for the first time in her life. "Benny! Benny, wake up!" she cried. But when she turned, expecting to find her husband on his feet, she found him still perfectly asleep, his chest still bobbing to a sleepy rhythm of breath. Alice turned back to Mac who stood waiting, smiling.

"I've got a gun." Alice said, slowly backing away from Mac.

"No you don't." he chuckled. "And frankly it wouldn't matter if you did."

"What are you talking about?"

Mac paused for a moment. How to break the news to her? He had always had a flair for the melodramatic and when his eye landed on the glass of water sitting on the nightstand he simply couldn't resist. "Say." he said "I'm rather thirsty. Mind if I wet my whistle?" Mac's voice was even and cheery as he nodded to the glass.

"What?"

"Been ages since I had a sip of—" Alice watched as Mac reached for the water. He curled his fingers around the curved glass and pulled, but when the object should have lifted, it remained stuck to the table. Mac tugged and tugged, theatrically using one hand to pull the arm with the hand gripping the glass. But nothing happened. It wouldn't budge.

"What a drag." Mac said, feigning surprise for a moment while continuing to tug at the undisturbed glass. "Guess that's why I always feel so parched."

"What's going on? Who are you and what are you doing to that glass and Benny!—" Alice ran around to the opposite side of the bed, putting as much distance between herself and Mac as the bedroom would allow.

"Alice. I know you're probably very confused and you've got lots a questions."

"How do you know my name? Benny!" Her voice turned from aggressive to pleading as she jabbed at the lump under the duvet but he remained asleep, entirely un-phased by the midnight charade.

Mac took one slow step closer to Alice. "There will be plenty of time for all of your questions, I can assure you—"

"This is a dream. This has to be a dream." Alice said, finding the logic. "How do I wake up?" She ran over to her body lying on the bed and began tapping the sides of her face, praying for consciousness.

"Alice. This isn't a dream. And that isn't you lying there in that bed." Mac kept his eyes on Alice and took another slow step toward her.

"That *is* me!" Alice said, jabbing her finger with each word in the direction of the body lying next to her husband. "*That is me.*"

"I understand your confusion." Mac said, holding up his hands. "I really do. But that's not you. That's just your body. It's actually not even your body now, just *a* body. A husk."

"Am I hallucinating?"

"Alice—"

"Is this because of that muscle relaxant I took last night?"

"Alice—"

"I told Benny those things do weird things to

me but he never—"

"Alice." Mac's voice was firm but kind. "You're dead."

Alice's face dropped and she stared at Mac. When she didn't say anything Mac looked down at Roo who stared back up at him. "What?" Mac mouthed, defensive, as if Roo were accusing him of being too blunt. Mac shrugged and turned back to Alice.

"I'm... dead?" she finally said.

"You're dead." Mac nodded.

"But how?"

"You died."

"I died?"

"Yes. You died. Heart attack it seems. And this is the afterlife, or whatever comes next. Or whatever you want to call it. A new chapter, if you will.

"My *house* is the next chapter?"

"Well, it's *your* next chapter. And mine. And the next chapter for everyone else who's happened to die in this house." Mac waved and headed for the door. "Come on downstairs. I'll introduce you to the gang." At the door he turned around and wasn't surprised to find Alice hadn't moved an inch. Instead, she stood staring at Roo. "Has that Golden Retriever been here the this whole time?"

"He sure has." Mac grinned. "Meet Roo." he said

and spun on his heel. "Take your time, Alice." he called over his shoulder and sauntered down the hall. He no longer tried to be quiet and let his polished brogues clack as he walked down the stairs with Roo trailing at his ankles. "Whenever you're ready."

He wasn't worried. He knew she would join them eventually. What other choice did she have?

CHAPTER 2: ALICE
Introductions

I stood in the middle of my bedroom unsure of what had just happened. I didn't believe it. Any of it. I couldn't be dead. Maybe it was a dream? Or more likely a mental breakdown? That's what twins under the age of ten will do to a woman. It was my brain playing tricks on me, not my body throwing in the towel. I was 36. I was healthy. I couldn't possibly be dead!

I walked over to the water glass the man had failed to lift. I hovered my palm just above it and closed my eyes. I breathed. "You're being ridiculous. This is irrational. Just pick the glass up, turn the light out and go back to bed you stupid woman."

I opened my eyes, ready to get on with it. I gripped the glass, pulled up and felt my stomach drop. I screamed and jumped back from the glass, rubbing my hand as if it had burned me. I stared at the object. It was like it had grown roots or something.

I turned to look at Benny who remained happily asleep and rolled my eyes. He had always been able to sleep through anything. Even, it turned out, his wife's death.

I marched back to the glass and wound up my arm, ready to use every bit of my strength to knock it off the table. I refused to die. I simply refused. But just as I had secretly suspected, and dreaded, the glass wouldn't budge. I swatted and slapped at the glass while my eyes reddened and I could feel tears prickling at the inner corners.

I stood back, breathing heavily and feeling helpless. My death was supposed to be an event. I was supposed to go out with a flourish and people were supposed to know, without a question, that it had happened. I was supposed to die doing something spontaneous, adventurous, important. Never mind that not once in my short life had any of those words come close to accurately describing me. But still, I was supposed to be *somebody* and my death was supposed to mean something. Surely, even for the Plain Janes of the world, death was supposed to be more than this?

I peeked around the edge of the bedroom door and looked both ways but the hallway was empty. I tiptoed down the stairs, examining every inch of the house on my way. I tried to spot the differences. It must've somehow changed, I thought, but how? I could still see the familiar scratches and scuff marks from shoes left on while hurrying back upstairs for that one forgotten item. The stack of laundry that had been folded a week ago and placed on the bottom step, waiting for a ride up by a passerby with a free pair of hands, was still there. I cringed to find that even the fine layer of dust that had been collecting in the space between each bannister rail remained. I bit my bottom lip. It looked the same. Exactly the same.

Standing on the final step, I paused. I could hear a murmuring to my left and figured that they, whoever *they* were, must be waiting in the living room. I walked and held my arm out, letting it lightly drift over the picture frames perched on the table and then the vase with the wilted daisies. I stared as my hand fluttered past the objects and felt fine until I came to it. Our wedding picture. It had been taken during our first dance and selected for the frame because we were both awkward in front of a camera and candid shots always did more for us than any posed, professional set up could. I ran my fingertip over the glass. My dress was long and lacy with a high neckline and Benny looked as handsome as he ever had with his dark hair and tortoise-shell glasses. I stared at the photo and could remember exactly what I had been thinking in that moment. It sounds cheesy but I remember thinking I couldn't wait to spend the rest of my life loving him. Without thinking I reached for the frame and when I couldn't pick it up a singular sharp spasm spread from deep inside my chest. It pulsed out to fingers and down to my toes. I stepped back.

We had bought the house eight months ago and had only been living in it for around six, but that was long enough for it to begin to feel like a home to me. My home. It had been long enough for it to become the place I wanted to be after a long day at work. Benny liked to call it our 'forever home'. That was what it was supposed to be. It was the home we were going to raise our twins in, and grow wrinkly in, and eventually downsize and sell because we were too old and the place had become too much house for two old folks like us. We would keep it and live in it and love it until it was time to pass it on to the next young family who would do the same.

"Why don't you join us in here?"

I jumped at the voice and quickly turned, officially torn from my world of nostalgia.

"Sorry." Mac said gently. He smiled and paused for a few seconds before continuing. "Come on in, Alice. We're friendly. Mostly. I promise." He smiled again and held his hand out to me like an adult to a reluctant child. I noticed his old-fashioned blue ruffled tux for the first time and thought he looked like some kind of ridiculous death concierge.

I followed Mac into the living room and found four people waiting for me, watching me. Five if you included the dog. It was more than I had been expecting even though I wasn't aware that I even had expectations.

"Well hello there. Welcome!" The voice came

from a small, wrinkly woman in a long floral dress who sat hunched in an armchair with a pair of knitting needles and a ball of yellow yarn in her lap. "Such a pleasure! Can't tell you how happy I am to have another lady round here!"

I nodded and smiled like I understood.

"That's Meredith Moss." Mac said, pointing to the old woman who smiled, picked up her needles and resumed knitting. "And beside her we've got Jeremiah."

The boy next to Meredith, who I guessed to be around twelve years old, gave a quick wave, as if his name had been called for school attendance. He wore gym shoes with thick, bunched-up tennis socks, red gym shorts and a bulky grey hooded sweatshirt featuring a grainy, faded university insignia across the chest. Peaking out from just below the collar I noticed a deep purple smudge running in a straight line across his neck. Jeremiah quickly tugged the material up and over his chin, and used his teeth to keep it in place.

I nodded and said a quick and quiet hi.

"Then we've got Roo, who you already met upstairs." Jeremiah reached out and scratched between Roo's ears. "He's a bit of a family pet you could say."

"Hello, Roo." I said and smiled, to which Roo licked my hand. I took it as a good sign.

"And lastly, we have Dr. Peter Cassidy." I turned my attention to the man sitting in the antique rocking chair in the corner. I had always thought the chair was too unstable to actually sit in and I had really only bought it as a decoration, but somehow the doctor seemed to suit it. He wore a deep grey, slightly tattered three-piece suit and sat with one leg neatly crossed and dangling over the other. At the mention of his name he looked up and nodded once before returning to his thoughts. "Don't mind him." Mac said. "He doesn't talk much. Silent sort of type."

"Right." I said. I nodded and fidgeted with the sleeves of my pajamas and realized I had never felt more uncomfortable in my own home.

"So." Mac collapsed onto the sofa. "Got any questions for us?"

Any questions? I thought. What does he mean *'any questions?'* That was it? That was the big explanation?

"Um. I'm sorry." I exhaled, loud and slow. "I just need some clarification. I'm not sure I understand... I mean, what's happening... Well, are you all... ghosts?"

"Sure, if that's what you want to call it. But we generally like to keep it a bit more open to interpretation."

"Okay." I said, confused. "So what do you call yourself?"

"Well, like I said it's, Meredith, Jeremiah, Roo, Dr. Peter Cassidy and me, Mac." Mac used his finger to point at each individual as he listed off all their names. "But no need to get it down-pat this second. You've got plenty of time, little Miss." The ease and calm with which Mac spoke unnerved me. Why was he acting like this was normal when it was the furthest possible thing from normal. The opposite of normal.

Though I felt like I had thousands of questions, I found it difficult to zero in on any one strand of thought and even more difficult to string together words in any sort of meaningful way. I could feel Mac watching me, standing awkwardly in front of all these new people, struggling to grasp what had happened and where to go next. He took pity and threw me a lifeline.

"Look." Mac said. "It's a lot to process, we know that."

Meredith nodded and let out a soothing mhmm sound.

"Here are the main things you need to know." Mac held his hand out in front of him and lifted a finger for each point. "One: You're dead. Two: everyone else in this room is dead. And three: All of us, at one time or another, died in this house and so we stay in this house." Mac paused, allowing me to absorb the information that seemed so simple but felt impossibly confusing. "All good?"

"For how long?" I said, proud of that fact that my three words had come out in the correct order.

"Well we've all been here different lengths of time. The house has been around since the turn of the twentieth so it's got some years under its belt."

"Believe it or not I'm not the oldest one here." Meredith chimed in. "Only been here two years." she smiled.

"Sure, but you lived in this house for more years than all of us combined—"

"I meant how long will I be here for?" I said. I didn't care that I was interrupting.

"Well…" Mac's voice trailed off and I watched the others avoid his attempts to make eye contact with him. Even Roo looked away.

"Nobody really knows."

"So this is…forever?"

"Yeah. Well, maybe. Or at least until whatever come next."

I walked over to the sofa and dropped down next to Mac. I exhaled and tired to pin down another question.

"So what's the deal with objects?"

"Objects are as real to us as the floor." It was Jeremiah who spoke this time. "They're barriers. We can feel them, touch them, sit on them" He patted the couch. "But we can't move them."

"That' right." Mac said. "That's why I couldn't pick up the water glass upstairs, and you couldn't pick up the picture frame. They're solid. Feels like they're glued down or something."

"Well, why does she get knitting needles? And yarn?" my voice sounded more accusatory than I meant it to.

"I died with them." Meredith said. "Apparently that means I get to keep them." Her smile was smug, as if she had won.

"And what about doors. How could you open the door upstairs?"

"Hinges. Crafty little things, don't you think?" Mac said and smiled but his face dropped when he registered the look on mine that no doubt read, no, in fact I do not think hinges are crafty little things.

"Look." Mac said. "We don't get to make the rules. They are what they are and we've been here a while so we've figured some of them out. Or at least we think we have. And the longer you're here, the more you'll figure out, too. But honestly, the sooner you learn to just accept it, the better off you'll be."

I looked around the room and absently ran my tongue over my teeth. I could feel a thin layer of plaque and tried to remember if I had brushed them before going to bed that night and wondered how was I supposed to brush them now if I wasn't even able to pick up a toothbrush.

I was scratching at a splotch of dried toothpaste on my thigh when realization hit me. I looked around the room at everyone else, paying particular attention to their clothes.

"Yep." Mac said, reading my mind. "Unfortunately, what you're thinking is right."

"I'm stuck in these pajamas *forever!*"

"Unless you want to be naked." Meredith said with a smirk in Mac's direction.

"Meredith went through a phase for a while." Mac said, diplomatically. "We've moved past it."

I tried not to cringe at the thought but knew I had failed.

"But look at me." Mac said. "Not a great choice on my part. But I didn't exactly know what was going to happen—"

Jeremiah snorted at Mac's words, almost cutting him off with the sound. But when Mac paused and turned to look at him, Jeremiah had apparently found something very interesting to look at on the floor. I watched the two of them for a moment before looking to Meredith who raised her eyebrows and just slightly shook her head 'no'. As if to say, 'trust me, you don't want to go there.'

"What about food?" I said, hoping to diffuse

the strange tension that had suddenly sprouted. "What do we eat? And when do we sleep?" The questions came from the simple urge to change the subject, but now that the words were out of my mouth, I realized that I really was interested in the answers.

"Eating and sleeping are physical needs." Mac said slowly turning back to me.

"And since you yourself are no longer physical…." he shrugged and lifted his hands. "No need for em'."

I tried to remember the last thing I had eaten and was sad to realize it had been a pitiful, hodgepodge of a meal consisting of leftover steamed broccoli from the twins' dinner, some yogurt and about five handfuls of Doritos.

"Okay, so if you don't eat and you don't sleep, what do you guys do? I mean, okay I get it; I'm dead. But what happens now?"

"We wait." Jeremiah said. He had let the collar of his sweater drop from his mouth, but he continued to hold the material high on his neck with his hand. I could see a sodden, slightly darker half crescent on the collar where he had been chewing the material.

"Wait for what?" I said.

"For morning."

"What happens in the morning?" I asked and

when no one answered I looked around, waited. Finally a sound came from the antique chair in the corner of the room. The doctor cleared his throat, and everyone turned to look. Apparently his joining the conversation was an occasion worth noting.

"The morning is the time when your family will wake up." He paused and glanced down at his hands, neatly folded in his lap. It was the first time the doctor had spoken since I had come into the living room and his voice was raspy with disuse. "Wake up and find you, that is. Dead."

As the weight of the doctor's words slowly sunk in, I felt my brows scrunch together in deep crease down the centre of my forehead.

Of course they would find me. How had I not thought of that yet? Benny was asleep now and blissfully unaware of what awaited him when he woke, but how much time did he have left? How long would it take him to figure it out? And how the hell was I supposed to be here, watching it all happen?

CHAPTER 3: DR. PETER CASSIDY
You Don't Exist Anymore

Waiting for the body to be found had always been the worst part for Dr. Peter Cassidy. He had been in the house the longest and had, for better or for worse, been the one to receive each of the others. This would be his fourth time watching the family find their deceased loved one.

When Dr. Peter Cassidy died, nobody had been waiting to receive him. The house had been too new and it seemed as though he had been the first to die in it. Alice was in a way very lucky. She had a whole group of people here for her, to help her, to guide her. Dr. Peter Cassidy had had nobody. But he was happy to have figured it out on his own. He spent his life alone and he intended to spend his afterlife in just the same fashion. He was a man who liked to sit and think and then sit and think about what he had sat and thought about. His only agony was not having access to a pen and paper with which to write down his many, many thoughts.

The most difficult aspect of the morning would be the twins. Dr. Peter Cassidy never had children of his own, but as a pediatrician he had always had an affinity for them and it pained him greatly to see a child affected, in any sense. Casey and Charlie were six years old. They were healthy, charming children whom, it had become clear since the family had moved in, loved their mother dearly. They were never without her for long and on most occasions served as third and fourth legs.

Benny was a decent man. A solid husband. The reliable sort. But he worked too much and from what Dr. Peter Cassidy could tell he knew more about PhD dissertations than the importance of a proper dinner, bath and bedtime routine. Benny would struggle with the change. He would struggle with losing his wife and he would struggle with becoming a full-time single parent.

Alice had undoubtedly been too young to die. She had a young family and unfinished business. But Dr. Peter Cassidy thought it must be rare that one actually died with all of ones business finished. Surely there would always be just one more bow to tie, one more piece of the puzzle to nudge perfectly into place.

But of course, in the end, one couldn't plan for life. Or death for that matter. To Dr. Peter Cassidy, time was a funny thing. He noticed how time was a thing people assumed they were owed. And rightfully so, he supposed, it was what they were told they were owed. But he knew the truth, which was that nobody was owed anything in life. And that if they had to be owed something, it certainly was *not* time.

Dissatisfaction, prejudice, pain. These were the things worth betting on.

***

As the night slowly turned into the next day, Alice sat perfectly still and silent on the sofa. Everyone carried on as they always did. Meredith knit, Jeremiah chewed on the neck of his sweater, Mac scratched the space between Roo's ears and Dr. Peter Cassidy sat hunched in the corner. These were the type of folks who were used to doing nothing. Every so often a light murmur of chatter would break out, but Dr. Peter Cassidy noticed that Alice didn't join in. She just sat and stared straight ahead. And though everyone tried to behave normally and tried to be inconspicuous as they peeked over to check on Alice, they all knew what was coming and knew that all that was left to do was wait.

By 6:30am the mid-August sun had already risen a fair bit, flooding hot summer light through the windows. A two second flash of navy blue plaid and bare feet passed by in the hallway and Dr. Peter Cassidy was on his feet. It happened so quickly that if he had been looking down or even had his head tilted slightly in the opposing direction, he would have missed it. The sudden movement, particularly from a fellow who typically blended in with the wallpaper, sent a jolt through the living room, startling everyone. Even Roo barked, once.

Dr. Peter Cassidy wanted to tell them what he saw. Benny was up. He had just seen his dressing gown in the hallway. He wanted to say it was beginning. But as it sometimes happened to Dr. Peter Cassidy, the words simply would not come to him. So he pointed to the door instead and all eyes shifted in that direction.

Alice jumped to her feet and fled the room. "He's up. I need to see him." She was gone before anyone could stop her. It only took a few moments for everyone, including Dr. Peter Cassidy, to quickly follow her.

In the kitchen Benny stood at the counter scooping ground coffee beans into a filter. Alice stood beside him, watching him, reaching a hand out to touch his shoulder and then pulling it back. From the opposite side of the kitchen Dr. Peter Cassidy observed the scene, biting his lip the whole time. He prayed she wouldn't try to touch him. Of course, he understood that it was a natural human inclination. An impulse designed to bring one closer to the thing or the person one loved. Touch was connection. But if she tried to touch Benny she almost certainly would not like what she found. It was an anguishing aspect of the afterlife. To physically lose connection with a loved one. To lose touch.

"He doesn't know yet." Alice said, almost a whisper. She studied his face for signs of distress. "He doesn't know. He must think I'm still asleep." Alice turned back to the small group gathered opposite her. "How can he not know I'm dead! Didn't he look at me?"

At almost the exact moment that Alice turned back to Benny, Benny turned toward Alice and walked straight though her. Alice closed her eyes and sucked in a sharp breath of air and braced herself for whatever would happen. But nothing happened. When she opened her eyes Benny was behind her rummaging through the cupboard, looking for his favourtie coffee mug. For a fraction of a second Alice had been as close to Benny as she would ever be again, and yet, from the expression on her face Dr. Peter Cassidy could tell she had felt nothing. And in this case, Dr. Peter Cassidy knew that nothing was far worse than even the smallest of somethings.

He didn't want to tell her that eventually it would turn into something quite unpleasant. A pins and needles kind of feeling. And that as time passed by, the stronger the sensation would be.

Alice patted down her body, trying to understand how it could feel so solid to herself and yet, apparently, so non-existent to Benny. A sputter of laughter issued from the top of the stairs before Alice could question what had happened. The twins were awake.

Alice pushed through the group, bumping shoulders, proving her physicality in a way she no longer could with her family or any other living being for that matter. She ran up the stairs, taking two at a time. Everyone followed close behind. Dr. Peter Cassidy trailed up last. He feared he knew what was to come before it happened.

At the top of the stairs Alice paused. To the left was her bedroom and to the right was the twins' bedroom. A second spasm of giggles flooded Alice's left ear and her chest tightened. They were in her bedroom.

It was a weekend ritual that Casey and Charlie would wake their mommy up by sneaking into her bedroom and jumping on the bed until she finally woke, all the while trying and failing to stifle their giggles. It was an event that other mothers might have dreaded, instead opting for a bit more sleep, but it was a moment Alice truly seemed to savor. Dr. Peter Cassidy had watched these moments play out every weekend and what he once viewed as sweet now veered towards the horrific.

Dr. Peter Cassidy didn't need to see inside the bedroom to know that the worst-case scenario was currently playing out. Instead of following the others to the bedroom, he sat on the top step and cradled his head in his hands. It wasn't their fault. It was a game Alice had played with them countless times before. The children would think she was pretending to be asleep, just as she had pretended to be asleep countless times before. It wasn't their fault. They couldn't have known.

An ear-piercing scream rang through the house as Alice took in what was no doubt a disturbing scene. Dr. Peter Cassidy couldn't bare to face it. He didn't need to. His imagination had already crafted it within his mind. Casey and Charlie bouncing merrily in their matching pajamas. Alice's body bouncing, stiffening by the second. Dr. Peter Cassidy cringed to think of it, but couldn't manage to dispose of the thought. It wasn't their fault. They didn't know that the thing they took turns jumping over was no longer breathing, no longer a human being, no longer their mother, but a corpse.

The twins' giggles and merriment continued as Alice ran from the bedroom. She passed by Dr. Peter Cassidy on her way down the stairs and ran to the bathroom just off the kitchen. In the blur of movement he had seen the anguish on her face, noted the tears that had dripped off her chin and were dotted on her shirt, recognized the frustration and helplessness. Dr. Peter Cassidy had seen some troubling things in his time, both dead and alive, but in that moment he was hard pressed to recall a more tortured example.

Meredith and Jeremiah moved to follow Alice down the steps but Mac held his arms out.

"Leave her for now. Let me." Mac said and Dr. Peter Cassidy was grateful. It was the thing Dr. Peter Cassidy wished he had had the courage to say. One of them should be with her, he thought, but she didn't need an audience.

As Mac slowly walked down the steps Benny came around the corner holding two mugs of coffee, steam swirling from the tops. As they passed each other on the staircase Mac paused. Everyone paused. They pitied the man who thought he was about to join his wife and children. He appeared well rested and happy and had no idea what was coming in only seconds.

Dr. Peter Cassidy rose from his sitting position on the top step as Benny passed. He nodded his condolences even though he knew Benny could not see him and made his way down the steps. He knew neither Meredith nor Jeremiah would tell him to stay. He assumed they attributed a level of seniority to him simply for his having been there the longest.

He stood outside the bathroom door, curious, but not wanting to disturb them. He knew Mac was more capable of helping Alice in that moment than he ever could.

"Stand up, Alice." Mac said.

"I can't."

"Yes you can. Here, let me help you."

"Why?" her voice was small.

"Because you can't stay sitting on the bathroom floor forever."

"Why?"

Dr. Peter Cassidy prayed Mac wouldn't make some adolescent joke about the cleanliness of bathroom floors or about the view she would get, or about giving her family privacy. He didn't.

"Come on." Mac heaved Alice to her feet. "Atta girl. You got this. Come on into the living room. Take a seat on the sofa." Mac paused. "Alice?"

A second extended silence came and Dr. Peter Cassidy couldn't help but look about the corner. Mac stood behind Alice with his arms hooked under her armpits, her body nearly limp and her eyes staring into the empty mirror.

"Where am I?" she whispered, somewhat mesmerized by her lack of reflection. "Why can't I see myself?"

"Because, Alice…" Mac said and adjusted his grip. "You don't exist anymore." His voice was soft and he said the words with patience and kindness, as if he hadn't already said a version of them countless times before.

Dr. Peter Cassidy pulled back from the edge of the door and walked towards the living room. The antique rocking chair waited for him and he had plenty to think about.

What Mac had said was true. She didn't exist anymore. None of them did.

CHAPTER 4: ALICE
What The Hell Was That?

The ambulance arrived faster than I expected it to. I didn't realize they would still rush to retrieve a dead body. Maybe they didn't know I was already dead. Maybe Benny hadn't known when he called 911. Maybe he still had some hope.

It was only a minute or two after Benny had gone upstairs that Casey and Charlie were hurried out of the bedroom.

"What's wrong with Mommy?" Charlie asked as Benny led the twins down the stairs to the living room.

When they walked into the room Jeremiah and Mac popped off of the sofa, onto their feet and shuffled to the edge of the room. I knew it didn't matter if they touched a human, but still I could tell it felt oddly taboo to them, so as a rule everyone seemed to do their best to avoid it. Meredith stayed sitting in her armchair, but kept one eye on the humans, ready to move if and when necessary. I sat hunched on the floor with one elbow propped up on the coffee table. All I could do was watch.

Benny patted the sofa cushions and draped and tucked a blanket over both of the twins. He didn't answer their questions and when the doorbell rang, shortly followed by a quick rapping knock, Benny flipped the TV on and pointed to it as if to say, you know what to do. He told the kids to stay in the living room while he answered the door.

"Who's here?" Casey asked.

Benny didn't answer, just pointed to the TV again and closed the door behind him as he left the room.

I sat facing my children who couldn't see me. I had expected them to follow Benny out of the room but they stayed put on the couch, one eye on the TV and the other on the closed door. Maybe they had sensed something in his voice. Something that said p*lease listen to me this time.* Something that scared them.

I wanted to climb up on the couch next to them, scoop up one under each of my arms, pull them close and be there for them even though they had no idea I was so close. I wanted to tell them everything was going to be all right even though I knew they wouldn't hear it.

There was a small movement under the blanket in between the twins and I knew it must've been Casey reaching to hold Charlie's hand. She always did that when she was nervous. I pressed my lips together. I knew everyone in the room was watching me, waiting to see what I would do, how

I would handle it. I didn't have a clue.

I scanned each of the twin's faces. They were so similar and yet so incredibly different. I memorized the pattern of freckles across Casey's nose and smiled to see my own deep green eyes replicated in Charlie's.

And then I was gone. Without thinking I sprang to my feet and sprinted for the front door. I couldn't handle it and if I could just get out of this house and away from my family, the family that was no longer mine, I knew everything would be okay. I could vaguely hear someone following behind me, yelling something, telling me to stop probably. Mac, I assumed. Probably telling me that everything would be okay. But it wouldn't be okay. That was just something you said to someone who needed to hear it. But they were just words. They were as real as me, and according to everyone around me I wasn't real at all. This wasn't the afterlife. Or the next chapter. Or whatever he had called it. This was hell and I needed there to be an alternative.

I jerked the door open and with one leg already leaning out the doorframe, my body tilting forward with momentum, I realized I had made a mistake. Everything outside the house was gone and had been replaced by nothingness. There should have been grass and a driveway and my car should have been parked on the driveway and beyond that there should have been a road that led to other homes with cars and driveways and grass. Instead, there was nothing except the blackest black I had ever seen. It was cold and there were bitter gusts of wind accompanied by a vague whistling noise, like air moving through a chimney. There was absolutely nothing and I was falling directly forward, directly into it.

Just before my second foot was about to lift off the edge, I felt the plaid flannel of my pajamas tighten across my chest and something hauled me back inside. I slammed against the floor, landing directly on my shoulder, my head bobbing up and then cracking down against the hardwood with the fall.

The door slammed shut and it was silent. It was like it had all happened in slow motion and I braced myself for the pain of the fall. A searing, aching kind of pain, that would tell me a bruise was forming. Could I bruise anymore? Did I even have blood inside me anymore? I waited for it, but the pain never came, and when I opened my eyes Mac was standing over me looking down, somehow managing to appear intimidating despite his ridiculous tux.

"What the hell was that, Alice?"

I closed my eyes again and wished for the pain of the fall instead. I would've preferred it to the lecture on afterlife etiquette I knew was coming.

"Thanks for coming." The voice was choked

and came from behind Mac and me. Benny stood at the kitchen island, his forearms resting on the marble and his eyes on the vinyl zip up bag being maneuvered by two paramedics towards the door. Instinctively both Mac and I scrambled out of the way.

I hadn't seen him standing in the in the kitchen. Had he been there this whole time?

One of the paramedics asked Benny if there was someone he could call for him. Maybe a family member or something? Benny shook his head no and quietly thanked them while keeping his eyes on the inky swirls of the countertop. The men looked at each other and then both gave a quick nod of sympathy to Benny and mumbled something like sorry for your loss. For people trained specifically for these types of occasions I was outraged by their awkward bumbling and the fact that without even another word, they simply opened the door, pushed the lumpy bag on wheels out and left.

How could they leave him like that? Benny was still in his pajamas and robe and slippers and it somehow made him appear all the more vulnerable. I watched him continue to stare at the swirls. I would have given anything to know what he was thinking about in that moment. When he finally picked his phone up I assumed he would be calling a friend, or a family member. I was wrong.

"Yes, hello." Benny said and cleared his throat. "I'd like to speak to someone about putting my house up for sale. Immediately, please."

CHAPTER 5: JEREMIAH
Here's Charlotte!

Jeremiah couldn't believe how many small, stupid details went into planning a funeral. Like a guest book. What was the point of that? Who was that for? Obviously not the dead person. So then who was supposed to keep it? And how long does that person have to keep it for? It didn't seem like the kind of thing you could just throw out after a certain amount of time like a birthday card or souvenir tee shirt someone got you at the airport because they worried it would mean something not to.

As far as Jeremiah was concerned, couldn't you just say goodbye, put em' in the ground and call it a day? If you really wanted to burn some paper you could splash out on some pretty flowers so everyone had something nice to look at, but why bother with all the rest of the hoopla?

Almost immediately after they took the body away, Alice went into hiding. She said that since she couldn't leave, hiding was her only option. She said she couldn't watch her family grieve so she spent all her time in the unfinished basement where nobody ever went because it was a crap hole.

And Jeremiah didn't blame her for wanting to

get away from it all since it seemed that those kids were always crying. Crying during the day. Crying themselves to sleep. Crying at night. And they kept asking when their mommy was coming home like they hadn't already been told a least a million times that she was gone. Jeremiah thought the kids were definitely cute, but not a whole lot going on up top, ya know?

Jeremiah wasn't sure if it was a coincidence, but the day Alice went into hiding was also the day that the For Sale sign arrived. He saw her looking out the window, watching as they planted it in the front lawn. It was hard to tell what she was thinking. Was she glad Benny was selling the house so that she wouldn't have to be trapped in the same house as her family? Or was she sad because them moving away likely meant she would never see them again. He couldn't decide if it was worse to be a silent observer on the life she should have had, or just cut right out entirely.

Personally, Jeremiah was glad that they were leaving. As far as he was concerned, the faster the grieving family left the faster things could go back to normal. He was looking forward to meeting some new people and hoped for a big family with lots of drama and action. He wanted to have lots to see. He didn't want a single person with a cat.

The day after the For Sale sign arrived, Benny's sister Charlotte showed up. She was the kind of guest who showed up insisting that you needed their help even though they had never been invited. In fact, as far as Jeremiah could tell, nobody really knew how Charlotte had even found out about Alice's death. She just appeared.

Jeremiah thought she looked like a deflated balloon in the way that some people who used to be really heavy and then lose a lot of weight did. Her skin was creped and freckled and tanned a deep brown and even though it was summer Jeremiah thought she probably looked exactly the same in the dead of winter. Probably lived somewhere warm year round. Florida, maybe.

Charlotte had one of those big purses slung over her shoulder that was more of a bag than a purse. The kind of thing that stored her wallet but also about a million other mostly useless items. From its depths she pulled a fist full of bars and rained them down on the twins, which Benny immediately protested against, thinking they were candy. But they were healthy, Charlotte told him, and continued digging in her bag for more treasures for the twins. Jeremiah peeked at the flashy label splashed across one of the bars. It was called "The Not Chocolate Bar!", which he guessed was meant to sound appealing but mostly just confused him. These kinds of things didn't exist when he was alive. Back then it was either a chocolate bar or it wasn't. Period.

Jeremiah watched the excess skin on her arms loosely wiggle as she reached out to pull each of the twins in a mushed up kind of hug. Weightlifting was what she needed if she wanted to do something about that. If he were still alive he'd have been happy to sit her down to discuss the pros, the cons and the expected outcomes of a regimented lifting routine.

For two whole years Jeremiah cut grass in the summer and shovelled snow in the winter. He saved every cent and slowly, with just one corner of the basement that his father had agreed to give up, Jeremiah constructed a makeshift gym for himself complete with a bench, free weights, and bar. When he wasn't in his gym he poured over every shred of information he could find on the greats of his time, the real pioneers of bodybuilding like Vince Grionda, Reg Park, and Steve Reeves. He wanted to be the best and at only 12 he had a work ethic like no other kid around. He was well on his way. Or at least that was what everyone always said.

Even after dying Jeremiah kept up his fitness routine. His weights were gone and even if he still had them he wouldn't have been able to pick them up. But that was just an excuse. Instead, he created a circuit based entirely on bodyweight exercises like pushups and sit-ups and all the other 'ups' he could think of. He did his circuit every day. And since he was dead and never got tired he'd sometimes do it two or three times in a day. He knew that he couldn't actually change his body anymore or achieve any real kind of results from his effort, but it was still a comforting habit to him. And if nothing else, it helped pass the time.

***

Alice stayed locked up in the crap hole basement until the day after Charlotte arrived. There was a whole lot of ruckus going on and Jeremiah couldn't blame her for wondering what it was all about. Charlotte had started her project while Benny stepped out for an appointment to finalize funeral details. He didn't want the kids to come so Charlotte agreed to let him go alone, although she didn't like the idea of it one bit and the second Benny had left she started pacing. It was like she didn't know what to do with herself or something. Jeremiah watched her peek in on the kids who were parked in front of the TV watching some brightly colored program and then quickly jiggle her way up the stairs.

Usually Mac would be there beside him, Meredith too if it was something really good. But Mac was in the crap hole basement with Alice, trying to convince her to come out and enjoy what little time she had left with her family, and Meredith had decided Charlotte wasn't worth her time. That only left the doctor, but it was virtually impossible to get a rise out of him and without even checking Jeremiah knew exactly where he'd be, legs crossed and thinking about one thing or another in his chair in the living room.

So Jeremiah followed Charlotte by himself. There was something about the lady that intrigued him. He had learned that most humans were predictable and found that he could almost always anticipate their next move. They unconsciously followed routines and left hints like scattered bread crumbs. It was boring.

But with Charlotte it was different. There was something about her that kept Jeremiah on his toes; he never quite knew what was coming next.

Jeremiah followed the sounds of Charlotte's rustling and found her digging through one of the two identical closets in the master bedroom. She had decided it was prime time to, as she would later say to Benny, 'cleanse the house of Alice'. Apparently it was 'all part of the natural grieving process'. Charlotte came out of the closet carrying a large load of assorted items on hangers. She didn't care to look at them piece by piece. What was the point? She clearly figured it simply all had to go.

Jeremiah sat on the bed watching Charlotte haphazardly pile Alice's clothes and shoes and belts and hats and bags onto the bed. Once the closet was empty she closed the door and began stuffing everything into big black garbage bags. She didn't even take the hangers off, just crammed them in along with everything else. Jeremiah stayed in his lounging position while Charlotte carried the bags two at a time down the steps, dumped them, and then thumped back up again. Charlotte was on her fourth or fifth trip when Mac stormed into the master bedroom.

"What the hell is that woman doing?"

Jeremiah sat bolt upright, as if he had been caught doing something he shouldn't have been doing. An accomplice of some sort.

"I said what is she doing?"

"Yeah, I obviously heard you the first time."

"This is going to kill Alice. I finally convinced her to show her face and now she's going to come up to find this shit going on?"

"Why did you ask if you already knew the answer?"

"What?"

"You clearly already knew what Charlotte was doing. So why did you come barging in here asking me what the hell was going on?"

"Jesus Jeremiah. Really? You're going to be like that right now?"

Jeremiah shrugged. Why couldn't he be like that right now if he wanted to? "What's the big deal? It's not like I could stop her if I wanted to. I was just watching. Someone should always be watching, don't you think?" Jeremiah held Mac's stare. "You know, just in case something happens." Jeremiah's face was hard, angrier than a 12 year old's face should ever know how to be.

"Whatever." Mac said, his voice a passive grumble as he rushed out the door.

CHAPTER 6: ALICE
Everything Will Be Okay

All my stuff was in bags. I had been dead only three days and already all my stuff was in bags. I knew it was my stuff because that stupid woman couldn't be bothered to take the hangers off of anything so they poked through the thin black plastic, offering glimpses of me and my life. In the bag on the far right was my working self. The fourth grade teacher self. Colorful and casual. Closer to the middle was my cleaning the house self. All the shlepy clothes I wouldn't wear out of the house but couldn't bring myself to get rid of so I kept them all and occasionally wore them while mopping the floor in order to validate their existence. And next to that were winter clothes and next to that were fancy wedding-type clothes. And so the parade of who I used to be via the things I used to wear continued. My eyes scanned over the bags. It was too soon for this. Way too soon.

What more could I say? I hated her. I had never really liked Charlotte, but now, just in time for me to do absolutely nothing about it I could finally say it. I hated her. Excellent.

And she hated me too. I had always known it. Years ago when Benny announced our engagement to his family the news had been met with happiness from everyone, except Charlotte. I could have sworn I saw her jaw fall open when he delivered the news. I brought it up with Benny a few times and he always brushed it off. She loved me, he would say. But no matter how hard he tried to convince me otherwise, we both knew that Charlotte had always been rooting for Benny's girlfriend before me to make a come back.

I had never been happier, or looking back on it now, more smug, than the day I married Benny. I remember turning from the alter as Mrs. Benny Trager and smiling a tight, victorious smile at Charlotte on our way out of the church.

Any privacy I had had in the kitchen with my garbage-bagged belongings was limited. I had been hiding in the basement for the past day and a half and everyone was clearly very interested in seeing how I would handle this new event. I could feel them watching me and was about to turn around and tell them I was fine, *I hated her, but I was fine*, when Benny walked in through the kitchen door and suddenly all eyes were off of me and on to him.

Wherever he had come from had not been good. He looked white and clammy and his eyes were ringed with a vivid, sharp red.

"What is all this?" he said. "Charlotte?" He choked on her name, as if it tasted bad. He coughed and called again. "Charlotte?"

Charlotte waddled into the kitchen clutching two more overstuffed and stretched plastic bags. She was just in the middle of blowing a tiny bubble with her tiny piece of sugar-free gum when she saw Benny and stopped short. The bubble snapped.

"You're home." she said.

"What are you doing?"

"How was the appointment?"

"It was awful. Obviously. What are you doing?"

"Well it was never going to be easy. But it's a necessary part of the process—"

"Charlotte, what are you doing with my wife's things?"

Charlotte shifted her weight and continued to clutch the two bags. "I figured it was the next step in the—"

"Please god don't say process. Don't you understand? There is no process for this. There is no protocol for tragedy. My wife is dead and I have no idea what to do because how could I? I'm not supposed to know. I'm not supposed to have planned for this."

"Of course. I was just... I wanted to help with the..." Charlotte's voice was quieter than I had ever heard it before.

"I'm not ready for this." Benny said, head hung, his voice hardly a whisper.

Any normal person with a clue would've have dropped the stupid bags and hurried over to apologize and comfort him. Maybe make him a cup of tea. Something. But not Charlotte. Instead, she awkwardly watched him for a few seconds and muttered something like "okay" before scuttling back out the door she had come in, dragging the bags she had brought in with her.

The kitchen was silent. Benny stood with his head still bent down and two fingers pressed to the corners of his eyes. When he finally looked up and took a deep breath I thought he was going to be okay. I think we all did. But then his face crumbled like a castle made of dry sand, his shoulders slumped and his knees dropped to the hardwood. He fell apart the way you only allow yourself to fall apart when you think you're alone.

Staying somehow felt like a violation of his privacy. From the corner Meredith sighed and as if on cue Dr. Peter Cassidy led the others out of the kitchen. Mac and Jeremiah followed immediately but Meredith paused as she passed me and reached for my hand. She held it in both of her hands and squeezed it in that comforting I'm-here-for-you kind of way before gently letting go and following the others.

I turned to Benny. My husband. My best friend. I kneeled in front of him as close as I could. His face was a wet gloss of tears. I couldn't hand him a tissue or rub his back. So I sat next to him and did the only thing I could. I told him I loved him and that everything would be okay. And then I said it again. And again.

I don't know how long we sat together like that on the kitchen floor. I didn't notice when the windows dimmed and the sun went down. Time was suddenly an irrelevant construct. I focused everything I had on Benny and I never stopped saying it. Reminding him. *I love you. Everything will be okay.*

And as I said the words I wasn't sure exactly who I was trying to convince more.

CHAPTER 7: MAC
Longer Than You Think

Dr. Peter Cassidy sat in his corner chair as usual while Jeremiah sat on the couch with his back to Mac, trying to physically demonstrate how much he was ignoring him. Mac left Jeremiah to his sulking and stretched out on the floor with his hands behind his head, as if looking up meant more than staring at a white, plaster-speckled ceiling.

Just before 2AM Alice slowly padded into the living room. Mac and everyone else had been waiting for her, not wanting to hurry or push her.

"Come now, Dear." Meredith said and patted the space next to her.

Alice dropped onto the couch and let her neck roll back to the meet the cushion.

"Tough day." Meredith said.

"Tough day." Alice nodded. "I'm exhausted. How can I be dead and exhausted?"

Meredith chuckled. "Seems unfair, doesn't it?"

"Mmm."

Alice paused for a moment. "I hope the house sells soon." she said to no one in particular. "That sounds terrible, doesn't it?" The room was silent

"I know I should want them to stay for as long as possible but I don't know how much longer I have in me. It's like they're being dangled in front of me. I can see them, but I can never have them. It's the most painful and frustrating dynamic. Ever."

Trust me, there are worse. Mac almost said but didn't. He didn't want to take away from what Alice was going through or disrupt her grief. But also, he didn't want to have to explain himself.

Ever since Mac yelled at Jeremiah in the master bedroom for 'letting' Charlotte bag up all of Alice's belongings, Jeremiah had been freezing him out. It was a pattern of Jeremiah's that Mac had grown used to. Right now Jeremiah was in the you-don't-exist-to-me phase of his freeze out and it was pretty much exactly what it sounded like.

Mac had said he was sorry, of course he was sorry. But sorry didn't seem to stick with Jeremiah anymore. It hadn't for years now.

But it was okay. Mac understood and had come to terms with it. He would wait it out and eventually Jeremiah would come around, realizing it was easier to forget than it was to remember. And the cycle would reset itself until Jeremiah found another trivial tiff to blame his everlasting resentment on.

***

The night slowly turned to morning and the day of the funeral arrived. The humans sat around the kitchen table wearing black and pushing soggy puffs of cereal around in their bowls, absently mashing pieces with the backs of their spoons. The only one talking was Charlotte who tried to fill the silences with something other than sadness. It didn't work, but Mac thought it was nice of her to try.

Alice stayed in the living room all morning until the front door clicked shut and Mac told her they were gone. She wasn't ready to see them again. Not after yesterday. He thought a little more time would help her collect herself, but when he went back into the living room he could tell that nothing had changed.

"Okay." he said, with a loud clap of his hands. "You've got about an hour and a half until they get back. Two hours, max. So you better do what you need to do to get ready now before they get back." Mac said.

"Like what? It's not like I could jump in the shower or get changed. Pajamas it is." Alice said with zero enthusiasm.

"That's not what I meant. I mean you need to mentally prepare yourself. In no time this house is going to be packed with folks milling about talking about you, grieving for you and your family. How are you going to handle that?"

"Who cares?"

Mac was sick of this side of Alice. Non-reactive. Uninterested. He wanted the Alice who always had another question, the Alice who was emotional and compassionate. Her shift irritated him. Couldn't she tell that he was trying to help her?

"Who cares? Don't you understand that this is likely the last time you will ever see these people? And then after that the house will sell and Benny and Casey and Charlie will move away and you will never see them again either. Doesn't that mean anything to you? All of your family will be gone. You owe it to them to be present today."

Alice stood and turned to leave. He wondered if he had gone too far but couldn't stop now. The words kept falling out of his mouth. "And I swear to god Alice, if you go hide in that stupid basement all day you'll regret it. I won't be coming down there to drag you out this time. If you can't bring yourself to show up today you'll never forgive yourself and if I can promise you one thing it's that forever is a lot longer than you realize."

Alice stared at Mac. He felt her eyes scan over him and knew exactly what she was thinking. It was hard to take someone seriously in a blue ruffle tux, but he hoped he had pulled it off. Forever really was a long time to carry the weight of regret and if he could help Alice avoid it he was certainly going to try.

CHAPTER 8: ALICE
White Roses

At first there were only a handful of people, but then all at once it seemed that the house was heaving. For a while I stood in the corner of the kitchen and watched familiar faces mill about in black clothing, clutching rumpled tissues in one hand and a toothpick-speared cheese cube in the other.

It seemed that every surface was covered in food and I had no idea where any of it had come from. There were platters of all varieties, and bread and cake and casseroles and booze and then more cake and then stacked up in boxes against the wall was even more booze.

I walked through the guests, catching snippets of their conversations as I passed by. They talked about me and my life and my family. *What a tragedy. She was so young. We never saw it coming.* I had never in my life had more attention focused upon me and at the same time I had never been more invisible.

I scanned the faces and recognized most. Our neighbors, our friends, extended family. I felt ridiculous in my red plaid pajamas and even though it was my own funeral reception and I was the guest of honor or whatever, I felt out of place.

The door to the spare bedroom was cracked open and I thought that, just for a few minutes, I'd go be alone. I had expected the room to be empty but when I walked through the door I found two people sitting on the edge of the bed, silent, dull, holding hands. My parents. How had I forgotten about them? How was it that this was the first time that it had even occurred to me to think about them? To consider how they had taken the news. I wondered if they felt the same as I did being away from the twins.

Dotted around the bed were the tattered trash bags filled with the contents of my closet. It seemed that they had been stashed in here to be dealt with at a later date.

My parents didn't say anything. They simply sat holding hands and staring at the off white carpet.

"I was going to tell you they were in here."

I turned to find Mac standing behind me at the door.

"You can't help them. They just need to work through it on their own." he said.

"I know." my voice was quiet.

"Do you want me to leave you?"

I shook my head no and before I realized what was happening Mac was beside me, one arm firmly secured around my shoulder.

"Take your time." he said.

I nodded and reached one arm around his back and half hugged him.

I didn't want to remember my parents this way. The black. The sadness. I wanted to remember them the way I would have had I still been alive. I wanted to remember the times I spent jumping on the trampoline with my dad as a kid. And the summer camping trips in the green tent with the patched up hole that always leaked. And Sunday morning breakfasts of pancakes and freshly squeezed orange juice and the jokes my dad would make about all the muscles he had from making the oranges juice and all the witty remarks my mom would follow up his comments with.

When I thought of my mother and my father I wanted to smile.

***

When Mac and I rejoined the reception, there seemed to be even more people than before.

"I don't even know some of these people." I said, scanning the faces. "A lot of these people actually."

"They're likely friends of folks who knew you. Funerals aren't just for the dead."

"Yeah but they didn't even know me. Like not even a little bit."

"Doesn't matter. It's about respect and support for the living."

I continued to scan, keeping a metal tally of people I knew and people I didn't. The people I knew were winning when my eyes landed on a woman standing awkwardly in the corner. I had never seen her before and immediately began guessing who she was and why she was in my house. Exactly who's friend of a friend was she?

The woman had short wavy hair and was pretty in a nondescript, hygienic kind of way. She wore a black tee shirt, black trousers, a black blazer and flat black shoes. She held in her hands a large, bouquet of white roses. I guessed she was close to 50.

I was ready to move on to the next guest, hoping to find someone I recognized to level out the tally when I heard Benny's voice.

"Colette." Benny weaved through the crowd. "Thanks for coming." he said and reached to hug her but quickly put his arms down when he realized she had put her hand out to shake.

"Yikes." Mac said and without looking I knew both of us were cringing. It was almost too awkward to watch. Benny shook the woman's hand and stepped back, hands in his pockets, nice and safe, where they belonged.

"How are you holding up?"

Benny shrugged his shoulders.

"As well as can be expected I suppose." she said and handed Benny the roses.

"Alice would've loved these."

"I'm glad." her smile was sincere.

A few silent seconds passed before either of them spoke. Benny had something to say and the woman was patient with him, letting him take the time he needed. The woman reached her hand out to Benny's arm and squeezed it gently.

"Who is that woman?" I said, unintentionally whispering.

"Shhh!" Mac swatted his hand in my direction as he narrowed his eyes on Benny and the mystery woman as if that somehow aided in his hearing or his understanding their conversation.

"People keep telling me it will get better, but I don't know if I believe them. I mean, does it actually get better?" Benny finally said. His voice quiet and choked.

"Eventually." she said, her hand still on his arm.

Benny pressed his lips into a tight line and nodded.

"She looks like a therapist or something. Do you think he started seeing a therapist?" I said, still whispering.

"Shhhh!" Mac swatted at me again. I smiled, amused by how seriously he took the business of eavesdropping. But it was too late, the conversation was over, or at least it would be over very soon. I could see a pile of frizzy, over-sprayed hair moving through the crowd and could hear Charlotte calling out Benny's name. It wouldn't be long before she found him and interrupted everything.

"Benny! Benny I gotta talk to you! Benny!" When she reached him she clasped her hands on his shoulders and jerked him backwards. "I gotta talk to you. Now."

Benny shrugged his sister's hands off of his shoulders and turned to face her.

"What is it? Are the twins okay?"

"Not unless you come with me right now." Charlotte said, deadpan.

"What's going on?" Benny said.

"Just come with me." Charlotte tugged at his hand and hauled him away from the woman.

"Thanks again for coming, Colette. I really appreciate it." Benny said with a small, still incredibly awkward wave.

The woman nodded and waved back. She watched him move through the crowd with Charlotte until they had both disappeared before quietly exiting back out the door she had only minutes before come in through.

Mac and I quickly followed Charlotte and Benny and from his perch on the stairs Jeremiah had seen the commotion and decided to follow, too. Charlotte opened the door to the pantry, looked both ways as if about to cross a road, and walked in, pulling Benny behind her.

We looked at each other, knowing the door would close soon.

"Ah to heck with it." Jeremiah said and hurried in just in time for the door to close behind him.

"What a little shit." I muttered.

"I can hear you!" Jeremiah said through the door.

I looked at Mac who was smiling, clearly amused.

"Oh. Sorry."

"It's okay. I kind of am little shit." I could hear Jeremiah's smile through the door.

"He's practically already sold it!" It was Charlotte's voice. Mac and I pushed our ears up against the door to listen. "I saw him over there talking to some pair of high heels about the 'original wood moldings' or whatever. You need to put an end to this. Today, Benny."

"But that's what I hired him for. He's doing his job."

"Really? Cuz from the looks of that helmet

you'd think his job was hair gel. I bet it cracks if you knock on it."

"Jesus, Charlotte. Seriously?" The door handle shook for a moment then stopped.

"He can't sell this house! You can't let that slick suit sell this house! This is your children's home; don't take that away from them."

"They're too young to understand all this."

"They understand that mommy isn't coming home. And they understand that soon they won't have a home. What more do you need them to understand?"

"That's not fair, they'll have a new home. Kids are adjustable."

"But this place is perfect. You can afford it on your own, it's close to the school and to the university for you. And lets face it you got this place for a steal. You think they're just handing them out like that these days? No sir."

"We bought it six months ago."

Charlotte paused, but only for a second. "If you go through with this, you'll regret it Benny. This is a mistake. I know it." Charlotte's voice was low. Benny was silent and I worried that even a word of her diatribe might have resonated with him.

"I have to get back." He finally said and pushed the door open. Mac and I quickly scooted back to avoid him passing though us. I looked at Charlotte, still standing in the pantry. She continued staring at Benny as he walked off and rejoined the guests. A bag of Flaming Hot Cheetos slid off the top of a precariously stacked pile of snacks and landed at her feet. She picked them up, opened the bag and dug her hand in.

"You'll come around." She mumbled between powdery fluorescent orange crunches. "You always do."

CHAPTER 9: MEREDITH
He Vanished?

"I can't believe that ridiculous woman convinced him. How! How?" Alice had been pacing the living room, repeating a version of the same line all night.

It had only been about an hour after the last guest had left when Benny went out the front door and started kicking and prying and pulling at the for sale sign dug deep into the grass. Meredith hadn't bothered to get up to see the debacle, but Jeremiah had come back in almost immediately to fill her and Dr. Peter Cassidy in on the goings on.

"The only thing that was keeping me going was knowing that it was going to end. That they would go and be happy without me and leave me to, whatever, I don't know, be forgotten about or something."

Everyone had been letting her vent, but after hours of the same old thing, it was growing stale and tiresome. Jeremiah and Mac and even Roo had disappeared to who knows where long ago and even Dr. Peter Cassidy in his rocking chair seemed to be tuning Alice out. That left only Meredith. Poor Meredith.

"Why did I have to die at home? This house is

a cage and I'll never get to escape it." Alice said for approximately the hundredth time.

"At least you didn't die in a hospital." Meredith said.

Alice stopped and stared at Meredith. "What?"

"Do you have any idea how many people die in hospitals?" Meredith cringed. "I don't, but it must be oodles, right? And then what, they're just stuck there, with all those other people and in only their hospital gowns? No space to yourself? No knitting needles?" She said holding hers up. "No thank you."

Alice chuckled and Meredith eased, feeling she had finally changed the direction of the conversation. She continued before Alice could revert to her broken record.

"If you think about it, it's a bit of a luxury to have died at home. I wish my Archie had died here instead of in that stinking hospital. I'd have kept him here if I knew this afterlife business was headed my way. Heck, I'd have killed him myself if I knew it meant I could spend forever here with him."

Alice chuckled again. Meredith suspected she didn't realize just how serious she was being when she said it. She would've killed him. That's how much she loved him.

"Listen, I know how that sounds and all, but

it's true. Call me romantic, I guess. I just think it would have been nice to have some family here, to have someone I love here. Like the boys, you know? I know they're almost always on the outs, but they're brothers and at least they have each other. That's something."

From across the room Dr. Peter Cassidy tutted at Meredith but didn't open his eyes. Meredith smiled. It was his first contribution to any conversation all day.

"The boys?" Alice said.

"Mac and Jeremiah." Meredith said, her voice innocent even though she knew exactly what she was doing.

"Brothers?"

"That's right."

"How did I not know that?"

"Well it's not exactly in the welcome pamphlet."

"How come Mac didn't tell me?"

Meredith raised her eyebrows and inhaled. "We're all here for a reason, dear. It would be good for you to remember that."

At this Dr. Peter Cassidy opened his eyes and fixed them on Meredith.

"What is that supposed to mean?"

"Just that we're all coming to terms with

something."

"Well what am I coming to terms with? And what happens when I do?"

"I couldn't tell you." Meredith said. "That's something only you will know."

"But I don't have anything to work through. Trust me, my life wasn't that dramatic."

Meredith lifted her eyebrows again and pressed her lips into a tight line.

"How do you know this is what happens to people with unfinished business only? How do you know that not everyone who dies ends up in this kind of place?"

"We don't" The voice came from the opposite end of the room. "It's just a theory we have."

"It's more than a theory." Meredith said. "We have proof."

"We do not have proof."

"Yes we do, there was Pete! What about Pete?"

"We cannot confirm what happened to that gentleman exactly. And please, stop calling him Pete."

"Why? It's a great name – it's short and easy to remember. What else are we supposed to call him?"

"We will call him nothing. We did not even know the man."

"You did!"

"I did not. I simply saw him and then—"

"He vanished!" Meredith said, eyes bright, and turned to Alice for reaction.

The doctor groaned from his corner. Meredith wasn't going to let this one go. He stood and walked over to join the ladies in the chair nearest to the couch.

"What do you mean *he vanished?*" Alice said.

"Tell her, doc." Meredith said, lightly poking Dr. Peter Cassidy in the shoulder.

He frowned and brushed his shoulder. "Well, the truth is that there isn't much to tell." He flicked his eyes to Meredith, cold and unimpressed. "It was only a few days after I had passed that it happened. I knew there was another person or entity or something in the house but I did not know anything about it or him. You see, I didn't exactly get the warm reception you did. I had no idea what was happening and didn't know he was likely just like me. Anyway, as I mentioned, it was a few days after my passing when I decided to confront this being and just as I did, it was in the kitchen actually, he turned and looked at me for only a second or two, smiled and, well, as Meredith put it, vanished."

"But where did he go?" Alice said.

"That is something I have been trying to figure

out every day since."

"And?"

The doctor sighed and tossed his hands up in the air. He had nothing.

"As far as I can tell it has something to do with all that Meredith was rattling on about."

"It's the truth." Meredith said, slightly indignant. She may not have been a doctor but she knew she was right and she wanted Dr. Peter Cassidy to acknowledge it.

"The working through something bit?"

"It seems so." he said. "But it's just a theory. It isn't based in anything. It isn't grounded in any kind of actual fact."

"Fact, shmact." Meredith grumbled.

"So there's a way out of here?"

"Maybe. Potentially. Nobody really knows."

CHAPTER 10: JEREMIAH
A Nanny?

Jeremiah did his routine twice. He was unsettled and a bit of exercise always helped him take his mind off that.

He didn't want Charlotte to go. There was something about her he found massively entertaining and watching her make her way through the day was far more interesting to him than anything anyone else, dead or alive, said or did in that house.

But Charlotte flew home about a week after the funeral. As she had put it when she told Casey and Charlie, she had places to go and people to see. The twins cried when she said it, typical wimps Jeremiah thought, but Charlotte stayed firm and told them her work here was done.

Even Benny tried to stop her from going. "Can't you just stay for one more week? Just until the kids start up at school again?" he said while he watched her cram clothing into her suitcase.

"You didn't expect me to stay forever, did you?"

"No, of course not. I just—well to be honest I hadn't really thought that far ahead."

"And there's no need to big brother. I've got

Middle Ground

it all sorted out for you. The twins start back at school next week. All you need to do is drop the twins off in the morning with their lunches and pick them up on your way home from the job."

"But I can't leave work that early. I have classes and meeting and--"

"Relax big brother. It's just for the first week. After what you've been though I'm sure your fancy job can allow it. And after that, I've secured the perfect nanny for you." Charlotte said, beaming.

"A nanny? What about daycare or something? Isn't it easier?"

"A nanny really is the ideal situation, Benny. Someone to help get the kids up and ready and off to school."

Benny nodded.

"Someone to cook and clean and be here after school with them until you get home from all your important classes and meetings and what not."

Benny frowned at Charlotte's sarcasm but it was clear he liked the idea of it.

"And Blair is truly amazing. Honestly. I can't wait for you two to meet." Charlotte smiled and crammed her phone charger into the already overstuffed outer pocket of her suitcase.

"Blair?"

"The nanny. You know when you meet someone and you just hit it off immediately? That's how it was when I met Blair. Like a house on fire or whatever they say."

"Well then why not just start with the nanny right away?"

"On vacation at the mo. But trust me, Blair is worth the wait!" Charlotte pulled her suitcase off the bed and retracted the handle. "Now I gotta get to the airport and I can't teleport so are you going to drive me or not?"

"I'll get my keys." Benny sighed and walked out of the room.

The house had been unbearably boring lately and with Charlotte leaving Jeremiah knew it was going to get even worse so the idea of a nanny was exciting to him. The injection of a new person into the house was just what they all needed to shake things up a bit. But when he told the others of the news they were hardly excited. Alice was still coming to terms with the idea that Benny was no longer selling the house and by the lack of reaction he got when he told the group, it seemed like everyone else was, too.

"But this is a good thing." he said in the living room while everyone half listened at best. "It means forward motion. Progress. It means something new. Don't you guys want something new?"

Jeremiah could not have been met with a less

enthusiastic response had he asked the question to an empty room. Not even Roo lifted his head, just kept it resting on Mac's thigh.

The low mood was contagious and Jeremiah could feel his excitement deflating as a few more silent moments passed. Finally Alice piped up, a crease between her brows.

"I wonder where Charlotte found this woman." she said.

Jeremiah jumped to face her. Finally a bite. "I've been thinking the same thing!"

"She's hardly left the house while she's been here. I mean, when did she have time to source and vet a nanny?"

"She goes on morning walks." Mac said. "Maybe she met her there?"

"Yes!" Jeremiah said, thrilled that another had joined in, even if it was Mac. "Excellent point."

"She probably pinched someone else's nanny from around here." Meredith said over the gentle clinking of her knitting needles and the room filled with soft snickers. Even Dr. Peter Cassidy cracked a smile.

"When does she start?" Alice said.

"In about a week." Jeremiah said and smiled. He felt like it was Christmas. Everyone was excited, or at least half excited, and he couldn't wait to see what kind of person arrived. He was hoping for as close of a replica to Charlotte as possible and he thought his chances might be good with like attracting like and all that stuff. Fingers crossed, he thought. Fingers crossed.

CHAPTER 11: ALICE
The Gossip

I had been waiting for the right time to talk to Mac about the things Meredith and Dr. Cassidy said for a while. I had so many questions and he was the one I always went to for answers. But I knew I couldn't this time. I couldn't figure out why he hadn't told me about Jeremiah and I felt strangely betrayed by the omission. I knew it was none of my business and that Mac didn't owe me an explanation, but I still wanted one. Of course, instead of being an adult and simply asking him about Jeremiah, I went the opposite route and avoided him altogether. I became awkward and darted out of the room any time he walked in. He didn't say anything, but I was sure he noticed me acting so strange.

I passed the time with Charlie and Casey, and followed Benny around, hoping Mac would think I was feeling lonely and leave me be. For part of the day I even tagged along with Jeremiah because I knew Jeremiah was still mysteriously angry with Mac and that Jeremiah's anger was something Mac seemed to respect.

I thought about asking Jeremiah about it but decided against it. Talking to him about anything serious seemed odd to me. I knew he was technically older than me, but that didn't change the fact that when I looked at him I saw a 12-year-old boy looking back at me.

I didn't know what I would do when the twins started back at school and Benny was back at work and the house was empty, with no places or people for me to hide behind. I was taking it moment by moment, not thinking too far ahead.

That night as the twins fell asleep I sat in between their beds watching a pattern of stars and planets slowly drift across the ceiling and then repeat. I had seen the motorized night light in a window display a day or two before we moved into the house and bought it for the twins on a whim, thinking it might make their new bedroom more enticing. It was a hit and had been used every night since.

Before I died, I had never thought about grief in children. Probably because I never had a reason to. But now, sitting between their beds as they slept, it was all I could think about. I wanted to know if they were doing okay. Did they cry too much or not enough? Did they miss me? Did they even understand what had happened? Like really understand it? Can seven year olds comprehend death? Will it mess them up? Will Benny do enough for them? Will Benny *be* enough for them?

There were far more questions than I had answers for, and once again even though I was dead I felt exhausted. I looked at Casey and then at Charlie. They were both deeply asleep and at least for the moment, everything was okay.

I peeled myself off the floor, expecting my back and butt to ache when I stood but I felt nothing. I still hadn't adjusted to the nothingness of my own body. Its lack of physicality.

I found everyone lounging in the living room, as was the norm during the nights. As I took a seat my eyes caught Mac's for a second and flicked away, though I could still feel him looking at me. He sat on the couch, Roo's head in his lap and Meredith sat in her usual spot knitting something that seemed to resemble a sweater.

"I know what's going on, Alice." Mac said before I had even made myself comfortable on the couch.

"What do you mean?" I said, not looking at him, instead focusing my attention on Roo and scratching the patch just behind his ear that he liked so much. I could feel everyone's eyes on me, pretending not to be watching me.

"You're clearly upset about something." he said.

I didn't respond.

"And I know what it is. I get it." he said, his voice sympathetic.

I still didn't respond. How did he know I

knew? Had Meredith said something?

"But I promise it'll get easier." Mac continued. "You'll get used to having them around."

"What?" I said and looked up.

"I know you were sort of depending on the house selling so you could move on and it's a tough thing for you to accept right now. It's why you've been so distant." My skin prickled. "But I think with time you'll come to see it as a blessing."

Any sadness I had been feeling quickly evaporated.

"Right." I said. "Because you just *love* having your family around so much."

My eyes flicked from Mac to Jeremiah for only a second, but apparently a second was enough. *Now* he knew that I knew. And although I didn't take my eyes off Mac, I knew everyone was watching. Meredith's needles stopped clicking, Jeremiah's light jumping jack stomping faded. Even Dr. Peter Cassidy, I was sure, was paying attention.

Mac paused and pressed his lips together, thinking. That's right, I thought. *What are you going to say to that?* When he finally spoke his voice was as sharp as mine had been.

"Don't waste your time being angry at me for something I had no reason to tell you."

He was right. The rational part of me knew

that. But instead, I shrugged, stood and walked out of the room. But just after turning the corner I stopped and listened.

"What are you doing? Why do you always have to go and stick your nose in other people's business, old lady?" Mac said in the same, sharp voice he had used with me.

"She has a right to know the truth." Meredith said.

"Like hell she does."

"Easy, Mac." Dr. Peter Cassidy said from the corner.

"She's going to ask questions. She's going to find out eventually." Meredith said and I could tell she wasn't afraid of him.

"Well of course she will. I have no doubt about that, especially with you coaching her." I peeked around the corner and saw Mac run his hands through his hair and pace before stopping and pointing his finger at Meredith. "You want to tell her things about your life or his life or anyone else's life. Fine. But keep me out of it."

"Or what?"

"I'm not messing around here, Old Lady. I mean it."

"I think it's time you walk away, Mac." Dr. Peter Cassidy said.

"Oh calm down, moustache. I'm fine. Everything's fine. Just leave me out of your gossip."

I should have known what would happen next. Of course Mac would storm out of the living room. Of course he wouldn't burst on Meredith and then just sit back down again like nothing had happened. I shouldn't have been so surprised when he came flying around the corner and knocked me to the ground, but I was. And so was he.

"Come with me." he said as he stepped over me, not offering to help me up. Roo licked my face once before hopping over my legs and trailing after Mac. I followed them into the kitchen and found him waiting for me, sitting on one of the barstools, legs dangling and arms crossed. I knew I should say something but I didn't know where to start so I just stood there and waited. I felt like a child waiting for a parent's discipline.

"It's important that we're all on good terms here, Alice." he said. I had expected him to be angry but his voice was gentle. "Friends, preferably. But good terms at the very least." I nodded like I understood. "It can be so lonely here. We're all each other has." he paused. "We try to make light of it, or at least I do, just to make it more bearable if nothing else, but make no mistake. We're trapped here."

"Meredith and the doctor seem to think there's a way out."

"And there might be. But we don't know how. We have ideas about unfinished business or whatever you want to call it, but we're only guessing." Mac shifted on the barstool. "And eventually some of us will get there, no doubt. Others, maybe not." his voice trailed off and his eyes looked up to mine. "I know you have questions." he said with a smile. "I'm not sure I'll have an answer for all of them, but I'll try."

I smiled and he patted the bar stool to his left. I padded over and sat next to him, leaning my arms on the counter top. "And before you ask, because I have a feeling it will be your first question, I can't tell you why you're here. I wish I could but I simply don't know. Only you'll know that."

"But I don't!" I said, slightly desperate. "Like not even a clue."

"You will. Eventually."

I rolled my eyes and exhaled. It wasn't the first time I had heard it and I still had no idea what it meant. What could I possibly have to work through or get over? The most interesting thing that had happened to me was my own death and surely that couldn't be the thing I needed to come to terms with.

"Okay well what about everyone else? You've been here with them a while, at least one of them must know why they're here. Dr. Peter Cassidy? He must know."

"He probably does. But if that's the case I can guarantee he wouldn't share it with any of us. You think I'd have figured the guy out with time, but I swear every day that goes by he becomes more and more of a mystery to me. You could try asking him, I guess. He might tell you."

I snorted. "No way. I don't even think he likes me. I always feel like I'm annoying him."

"I don't think he likes anyone."

I laughed. It felt good to have an easiness back between us.

"Meredith is pretty open. She says she simply refuses to cross over because she knows all about heaven and all about hell and she knows where she's going and according to her it's not the same place her Archie went.

"She doesn't think her husband went to heaven?"

"No she does. She definitely does. But she doesn't think she will."

"Oh."

"She says she's quite happy to stay here. Says she doesn't really have a reason to move on from here."

A cough from the kitchen door caught both of our attention.

"Can I talk to you?" Jeremiah said, eyes on Mac.

"Yeah." Mac said but didn't move. "Of course." Jeremiah turned and Mac followed him followed by Roo.

I sat staring at the empty space beside me. I had gotten a little information, but nothing I had really been looking for. And sure, our conversation had been interrupted and maybe Mac would've eventually gotten around to Jeremiah, but I wasn't convinced. Why didn't he want to tell me about Jeremiah? What could be possibly he hiding?

CHAPTER 12: MAC
It's a Tradition?

Jeremiah wanted to know what Mac planned on telling Alice and when he told him he planned on telling her nothing Jeremiah simply grunted. He turned to leave like it was the end of the conversation but stopped himself.

"Did you know Benny is afraid of spiders?" Jeremiah said over his shoulder. Mac didn't respond and instead just stood and stared at his little brother, confused by the sudden change in the conversation. "I'm serious. He's got one trapped under a paper cup upstairs." Jeremiah paused. "Pretty funny, actually." he said and walked away.

Mac stared at his little brother's back as he sauntered down the hallway and disappeared up the stairs to no doubt check in on the status of the spider-under-the cup saga. *What the hell was that?* Mac thought to himself. With the way Jeremiah had been ignoring him lately he had been expecting a blow of anger not some amusing anecdote featuring the man of the house.

Mac ran his hand through his hair and shook his head, feeling like he had just dodged a bullet and not exactly understanding how. He figured his brother's unusually good mood must've had something to do with the fact that the new nanny would be starting soon. Jeremiah had been buzzing about it for days. He always got excited about these kinds of things. Someone new to distract himself with, Mac supposed.

Mac looked back in the direction of the kitchen, wondering if he should go back and pick up his conversation with Alice. He thought he had put her off the trail a little, but he knew she would be back for more information soon. And he knew if he said no it wouldn't just end there.

There were two other people in the house who could tell her the things she wanted to know, and he needed to make sure they kept their mouths shut. He felt confident that Dr. Peter Cassidy wouldn't say anything. Not because he was particularly loyal to Mac, but because he hardly said anything, period.

But Jeremiah was another story. Despite their recent bizarre interaction, Mac knew that given the right circumstances his little brother would spill the beans like he was being paid for it.

Mac decided to leave Alice alone in the kitchen and joined the others in the living room. He dropped onto the couch and let his head roll back to rest on the cushion. Roo Jumped up and nestled in next to him but Meredith ignored him and continued clicking away with her knitting needles. Mac lifted his head and looked over. Her face was stern and undistracted. He licked his lips.

Mac looked at the doctor who sat in the corner looking directly at him. It was rare to see him so keenly engaged in something going on outside of his own mind. Mac shrugged as if to say 'what?' The doctor nodded in Meredith's direction. Mac shrugged again. What did he want him to do? The doctor narrowed his eyes on Mac and nodded to Meredith once again, who kept her eyes focused on her moving needles. Mac released an audible exhale, his shoulders hunched down in the process. Then with a roll of his neck he turned to face Meredith.

"I'm sorry." he said like it fast, like it was one word. He looked back at the doctor who had simply raised his eyebrows. Not enough, they told him.

"Meredith." Mac said, reaching over Roo to take one of her hands in both of his. At first she didn't want to give it to him and kept knitting. "Meredith, please." Mac kept gently tugging at her hand and eventually she stopped and looked over at him.

"Yes?"

"Meredith, I'm sorry. The way I spoke to you was unacceptable." She nodded and pursed her lips. "But can you find it in your heart to forgive a silly boy like me?" his eyes shone. He had done this before.

She stared at him, pretending to think it over.

"Fine." she said and pursed her lips. "Just this once." But of course she knew that wouldn't be the last time. Mac might've been around since the 50s but the 17-year-old boy with the bad temper was still there inside of him. And though she knew that it had happened before and that without a question it would happen again, it was easier for her believe in something she knew to be a lie rather than face the truth.

***

Benny sat on one of the kitchen barstools eating toast and reading the paper. Under his robe he wore red plaid pajama bottoms that matched Alice's exactly.

"It's nearly 7am!" she yelled, arms crossed and staring at Benny. "He's acting like it's the weekend. Like he's got all the time in the world. *What is he doing?*"

"Seems to me that the man is simply enjoying a pleasant morning."

"But the twins aren't even up yet! If he doesn't want to be late to his first day back at work he'll need to leave in 40 minutes. 45 max."

Benny flipped the paper to the next page and refilled his coffee cup. Mac watched him slurp a sip and recoil, apparently unhappy with how hot it was.

"What are you doing?" Alice said again, getting a little bit louder every time she said it. Mac thought she might pull her hair out with the way she was running her hands through it. It was almost amusing to him to see how riled up she was getting.

"You need to calm down." Mac said, placing his hands on her shoulders, which she immediately shrugged off.

"Hasn't anyone ever told you that you should never tell someone who needs to calm down to calm down? It's about the worst possible thing you can say."

"So you admit you need to calm down." Mac laughed and Alice scoffed and rolled her eyes. He suspected that laughing wasn't a particularly good thing to do either, but he couldn't help it. "There is literally *nothing* you can do about any of this." Mac pointed to Benny who was wiping crumbs off his chin and shirt and then watching them fall to the floor. "It doesn't matter how wound up you get or how many times you ask him what he's doing. All you can do is watch. Or don't watch. Go join Meredith and the doc in the other room."

Alice looked like she was going to say something but paused instead. She exhaled and leaned back against the wall. "I know." she said

"Good. So just, you know—"

"Don't you dare say calm down."

"Okay, okay." Mac laughed. "How about, 'take it easy'." His tone was half a question and half an offering. Alice accepted it.

"Ah yes, finally!" Alice said when Benny finally closed the newspaper and stood from the barstool. "If he gets a move on, he'll only be a little bit late." Mac looked at her and motioned with his hands for her to calm down, to *take it easy.*

"It's out of your hands, Mama Bear." he said.

***

By 7:45am, the time that Benny and the twins should have at the absolute latest been leaving, the house was in a state of chaos. Charlie was running around with his pants on his head, refusing to get dressed. And Casey was screaming a high-pitched squeal-like kind of scream. Benny had told her to comb her hair and handed her the plastic comb Charlie used instead of the special hairbrush Alice had bought specifically to help with the knots in Casey's long, thick hair. The comb had become so thoroughly tangled in Casey's nest of hair that the bright blue plastic had almost disappeared entirely within the strands. She sat on the floor in a slump, face puffy and tear-stained and wailed while Benny tried to catch Charlie. The phone rang but Benny ignored it.

"Jesus Christ." Mac said. "This is bad." He had assumed things would be a bit hectic, but he had never seen anything like this before. It was absolute mayhem.

"Of course it's bad. I told you it would be bad." Alice said.

"It's like he's never done this before."

"He *hasn't*. I always did this stuff." Alice slumped against the wall. "It's their first day of second grade and they're going to be late *and* he's not going to take the picture. I know it. I always took a picture of them on their first day school. It was a tradition."

"Well, not really."

"What?"

"For one year you took a picture. I mean, they're only starting grade two, right? Which mean technically you only did it once so it's not really a tradition—"

Alice turned to Mac, her face tight and he immediately regretted the comment. "It was going to be." she said between clenched teeth. "You know, *before I died.*"

Mac mumbled something like sorry and they both turned their attention back to the action. Benny had finally managed to catch Charlie and remove the pants from his head, but now he was pretending to be asleep.

"That's one of his favourtie games. He pretends to be asleep and goes completely limp. It's impossible to do anything when he does that."

Jeremiah sat perched on the stairs, laughing. He was truly loving this. The doctor, Meredith and even Roo stayed in the living room, happy for a quieter start to their day.

"The trick is to tickle him. That's what he's waiting for." Alice said. "He baiting Benny but Benny doesn't know it."

The phone rang again and this time instead of ignoring it, Benny answered it.

"What?" he said, breathless and frustrated. "Yes I'm still here. Why would you think I wouldn't be here?" He put the phone on speaker, set it down and shifted his attention back to maneuvering Charlie's dead-weight legs through each pant leg.

"It was a test! And you, big brother, have failed." Charlotte's voice came through the speaker.

Mac saw Jeremiah straighten up at the sound. What was it about that woman that interested him so much?

"Charlotte, is there a point to this conversation other than to highlight my total incompetence? If not, I need to go."

"What have you packed them for lunch?"

"Lunch?" Benny paused.

"Mid day meal? Heard of it?"

"They don't feed them?"

"No, that's your job, Dad."

Mac could feel Alice shudder beside him. She lifted her hands to her head and massaged her temples as if she could feel a headache coming on even though he knew it must've been a force of habit. There would be no pain.

"Cash!" Benny said. "I'll just give them some money."

"What kind of school do you think they go to? They don't have a cafeteria."

"Well, then... we'll pick up something on the way." Benny said, focused on his task. He pulled Charlie's pants up to his hips. "There. That's one dressed!"

"They aren't even *dressed*?"

"No." Benny picked up the phone. "One is." He said and hung up, frustrated that she didn't share his elation in the complete triumph that was getting Charlie's pants on. Benny turned to Casey who had decided to dress herself in one of her princess dresses. She sat on the floor in a poof of blue tulle; comb still stuck in her hair, cheeks still puffy from crying, and dipped her finger in a family sized container of yogurt.

When Benny looked back at Charlie, he had kicked his pants off again and lay 'asleep'.

Mac turned, expecting to find Alice next to

him as she had been all morning, but she was gone. He wasn't sure when she had left.

Almost an hour later the front door slammed shut and everything was quiet. Finally.

CHAPTER 13: ALICE
Hi There! I'm Blair.

I couldn't stop thinking of the twins showing up to their first day of school with two grease-stained MacDonald's bags for lunch. It seemed unlikely that Benny would go that far, but after the morning I had just witnessed, nothing seemed entirely impossible.

Benny was an English Literature professor at the university. The mornings were his most productive time of day so he would often leave the house around 6:30AM in order get some work done in his office before the day officially began and things got busy, rushed and forgotten about.

I had always been the one to get the kids together in the morning, but it wasn't because I didn't think Benny couldn't do it if needed. It was just because it was what made sense in our house. I was a teacher at the school the twins had started first grade in last year. It was easy for me to take them with me in the morning. It just worked. It had never occurred to me that a time would come when I wouldn't be the one with these responsibilities.

By that evening things hadn't gotten much better. The kids burst through the front door, shedding their jackets and backpacks as they ran.

Benny followed, already looking tired.

He asked the twins what they wanted for dinner. Casey wanted pasta. Charlie wanted cake. Benny ordered pizza.

I'll admit that things did slightly improve as the week went on. Benny woke the kids up earlier and became less susceptible to their typical games. But by the time Friday evening came around, Benny looked exhausted. He fed the twins dinner, pizza again, and parked them in front of the TV with their favourtie movie. Meredith wasn't happy about it because it meant she had to move off the couch, but nobody tried to take the chair from her so she stopped her grumbling and settled back down. The rest of us sat on the floor and watched The Jungle Book along with the twins.

The doctor didn't officially join us for the viewing party, but a few times I looked over and caught him watching along with the rest of us. I wondered what year he had died. Had movies been invented yet? If so, how many had he seen? I wanted to ask him, and everyone else in the house for that matter, how they had died, but somehow it felt like a rude thing to ask. I felt awkward just thinking about it. Never mind the fact that they all knew about me and how I had died and in a way I thought it was only fair for them to tell me how they had died too.

I had expected Benny to join Casey and Charlie for the movie, but 45 minutes into it he still hadn't returned so I slipped out of the living room.

The light in the kitchen had been left on and dirty plates covered in crumpled napkins and half-eaten crusts were still scattered across the counter top. Two slices of cold, congealed pizza remained in the open box.

I found Benny in his office. I stopped at the doorframe. He sat at his desk holding a paper in one hand and a healthy whiskey in the other. As he read from the paper I stood and watched, just like I used to do. I'd wait for him to notice me and then I'd smile and ask if he was coming to bed soon. He'd smile back and tell me he was just finishing grading a paper and that he'd be in soon. I'd leave him be, knowing that 'soon' was a relative term spanning the scale of five minutes to a couple of hours.

But he didn't see me this time. Of course he didn't. He couldn't. He was too engrossed in whatever he was reading and I was too invisible. As I turned to leave I heard a small sniffle and turned back in time to see him toss his glasses on the desk and firmly swipe his hand across his eyes. He sniffled again and chewed his thumbnail, still staring at the paper in his hand. I walked around him and looked over his shoulder. He wasn't grading a paper. He was reading a letter I had written him the night before our wedding. At the bottom by my signature was a row of x's and a smudged bright red impression of my lips. I could still remember buying the shade specifically for the task, thinking it would be sexy or something. I still had it, somewhere. It had never occurred to me that the lipstick would last longer than me.

I wanted to wrap my arms around him and hold him, give him a backwards hug. But I knew if I tried my arms would pass right through him. I knew if I tried it would mean nothing.

***

It was Sunday evening and Jeremiah was buzzing. He had overheard Benny on the phone to Charlotte and apparently Blair the new nanny was hoping to pop over quickly that afternoon to meet Benny and the twins, as well as pick up a key.

And it wasn't just Jeremiah who was excited to meet her, all of us were. Or at the very least we were all intrigued. I have to admit that I wanted to see the woman who would be taking care of my children. There had been so much chatter about her. I wanted to size her up and decide for myself if she was good enough for my kids.

It was just after 3pm when the doorbell rang. We were all sitting in the living room and Jeremiah sprang to his feet at the sound, swiftly clearing about four feet of carpet between the couch and the place his feet landed. He disappeared around the corner before any of us had even stood.

"You coming?" I said to Meredith who kept knitting.

"Nah." she said. "I'm sure I'll meet her eventually."

I almost asked the doctor if he was coming but thought better of it and followed Mac out of the room. At the front door Jeremiah was hopping from one foot to the other, waiting for Benny to catch up and open it. The doorbell rang again.

"Coming. I'm coming." Benny said, half jogging. He opened the door and stood silent. We all did.

"Hi there! I'm Blair. You must be Benny. So nice to finally meet you!"

Benny paused. I could tell that Blair was not at all what he had been expecting. To be fair, I don't think Blair was what any of us had been expecting. Blair was a man.

"Yes, yes. Please, come on in." Benny said and stepped aside.

"Great." he said and offered a warm smile, the kind that showed his laugh lines and crinkles at the eyes. I guessed he was somewhere around 50, though it was hard to know for sure. He was clean-shaven and his skin was flawless. His hair was a shiny brown with hints of dark grey at the temples. And in crisp tan chinos and a pink and white paisley short-sleeved button down, his entire appearance was immaculate.

"He's nothing like Charlotte." Jeremiah said. And it was true. I had no idea how Charlotte had found him.

"I think we've got some visitors." Blair said and pointed to the end of the hall where two giggling faces disappeared around the corner.

Benny laughed. "Casey, Charlie, come meet Blair."

They peeked around the corner again and Blair waved.

"Come on, don't be shy." Benny said.

Charlie stepped around the corner first, smiling, and Casey quickly followed. They skipped to the space behind Benny and peeked out from behind his legs.

"What are you guys doing?" Benny chuckled. "This is Blair, he's going to be helping me out for a while. Please introduce yourself."

They both grinned but shook their heads no, lips glued together.

Blair crouched down, resting his elbows on his knees. "Your Auntie Charlotte has told me all about you two. I think she loves you very much." He looked to Charlie first. "You must be Charlie." He said, and held his hand out to shake. Charlie looked at it for a moment. I knew he knew what to do with it, but I wasn't sure he would do it. The twins had always been shy around new people. But without another word from Blair or Benny, Charlie reached his hand out to meet Blair's.

"Very nice to meet you. I hope we can become good friends." Blair said. Charlie nodded, a smile peeking out from his lips.

Before Blair could go through the same routine with Casey, she had pushed her arm forward, copying the gesture. "I'm Casey." She said. "I'm a minute and 34 seconds older."

"Are you?" Blair said, and nodded, impressed. He shook her hand.

"Can we be friends, too?" Casey said, half as confident as she had been a second ago.

"Of course we can." Blair said. "In fact, I'd like that very much."

In the kitchen Benny and Blair chatted about schedules and the logistics of the arrangement while Casey and Charlie pulled on Blair's arms, asking him if they could show him their new Lego set, and their cool bedroom, and if he had seen The Jungle Book.

***

The next morning when Benny came down the stairs, still trying to straighten his tie, Blair was already in the kitchen. The coffee already brewed.

"Good Morning." Blair said as he sliced in half one of the two sandwiches on the cutting board in front of him. I couldn't have been happier to see

Middle Ground

the twin's lunchboxes open and half-filled on the counter. Blair had prepared a lovely, healthy lunch for each of them.

"Morning." Benny said as he poured himself a cup of coffee. "What time did you get here?"

"Oh I'm an early riser." Blair said. "And I live just down the street so it took me no time to get over here." Blair placed the sandwiches in the lunchboxes and zipped them closed.

"Where did those come from?"

"Oh I found them in there." Blair pointed to the pantry. "Should I be using something else?"

"No, no." Benny said, surprised but pleased. "Those look good to me. Wish I had known about them last week." Benny paused. "It was a bit, uh, hectic around here last week. First day of school for the twins and first day back at work for me since-" Benny stopped. I'd never thought of how it would feel for him to address my death to other people. Even people who already knew about it. The awkwardness. The forced sympathy. The vulnerability.

"That's absolutely understandable. I'm happy to be here to help." Blair's voice was genuine and not even a drop patronizing and I suddenly felt myself feeling more grateful for Blair's presence in our home than I had felt for anything in a long time. Benny would come to like Blair more than he realized, I could already tell.

After weeks of tension and roadblocks it was nice to see something go so well, so smoothly. It was nice to see the kids so excited about something. Or someone, for that matter. I had a good feeling about Blair. He was so bright and happy and full of a kind of lightness that our sad home had not seen in too long.

CHAPTER 14: MAC
It Was Too Perfect

Mac knew things would work out with Blair when on his first day he lined the twins up just before taking them to school. Their uniforms and backpacks were on. They were ready, and early even. He told them to smile and took a picture of them with his phone and told Benny he would send it to him.

"It's important to have these kinds of things. The milestone pictures. The first day of any new year is a big deal and worth remembering." he said.

"But it's not our first day. That was last week." Charlie said.

"A technicality." Blair said with a wave of his hand. He tucked the phone in his back pocket and swiped the keys off the counter. "Time for school." he said and they were gone.

"Okay now it's a tradition." Mac said and turned to find Alice smiling, smug. She couldn't have planned it better herself.

"You know, before Blair came I didn't want to be here. I hated that they weren't moving and that I was trapped here. But now, I feel kinda lucky that I get to see this. It's like I still get to participate in a way, ya know? I wouldn't get to see their faces anymore. Where would I be? What would I be thinking? How would I know how they were doing? "

"You wouldn't." Mac said, simply.

"It's crazy to think about." Alice said. "Anyway. I'm going to go see what the others are up to."

"I'll be in soon." Mac said and was left alone in the kitchen.

He walked to the window. It was still only early September but a few of the leaves on the maple tree in the yard were already transitioning from their vibrant summer greens to shades of amber, rust and orange. That tree had been around since before Mac's parents bought the house and he had been watching it grow from the kitchen window for decades now.

It had been a few weeks since Alice's funeral and things were slowly getting back to normal. Or at least trying to shift into a new kind of normal. When most people thought of death they thought of getting the news, the reactions, the condolences, the funeral. But what about all the stuff that happens after that? Mac wanted to know why people didn't think about what happened after the mother or father or husband or wife or whoever it was that thanked everyone for coming and closed the door on the final funeral guest and had to turn around and deal with life. Nobody seemed to care about what happened when it was over and quiet and everything was just the same as it always had been but also painfully different. Why, Mac wanted to know, did nobody think about that?

Mac thought of his parents and how they found their dead sons. Jeremiah in the basement and Mac in the garage. His mother had run from the house, screaming like he had never heard another human being scream before. The sound was the most intense, most distinct expression of terror and agony that Mac had ever heard. His father fled the house moments later, following his wife. That was the last time Mac had seen either of his parents. Three days later a van full of boxes and four plump but surprisingly strong movers pulled up in front of the house and emptied it of every last item except Jeremiah's gym equipment.

A few months later a new family moved in as if nothing had ever happened. As if no one had ever lived there and it had only ever been theirs. It would be 28 years before another person died in that house and that person would be Meredith. But until then, the house would flit between ownership, casually moving from one family to the next while the doctor, Jeremiah, Mac and Roo merely existed in the background.

Mac often wondered about his parents. He knew that if he were still alive he'd be in his 80s so that meant his parents would be long gone. But he wondered about their lives and how they had turned out. Where did they go when they left? And did they ever manage to move on? Had they forgotten about him? Had they forgiven him?

And even if they had, which for the record he found highly unlikely, Mac knew he could never forgive himself. He wouldn't allow himself to. It was a conclusion he had reached decades ago and had come to terms with. It meant that he would never leave this house and that regardless of the escape theories, Mac knew there was no 'next' for him.

***

Blair had been taking care of the twins for almost a month when the first outburst happened. Mac wasn't sure how grief worked with 6 year olds, but he was sure it wasn't a black and white kind of thing. There would be good days and there would be bad days. Today was a bad day.

After school, Charlie rushed through the door, his face bright red, soggy and snot stained. Blair and Casey followed quickly behind him.

"What happened?" Blair asked Casey who shrugged her shoulders.

"We're in different classes. He was already crying when I saw him and he won't tell me why."

Blair nodded, his face tight with concern.

"What's going on?" Alice said as she walked

into the kitchen. "Charlie just blew past me in a total state and ran up to his bedroom."

"Kid won't talk." Jeremiah said.

Mac guessed that Alice was about to start screaming uselessly at Blair to go to Charlie and ask him what was wrong when Blair reached for Casey's hand and the two rushed after him.

Mac, Jeremiah and Alice followed closely behind. "Probably just a bad day at school, Alice. These things happen. Nothing to worry about, I'm sure." Mac said, trying to be reassuring or comforting though he wasn't sure Alice had even heard him. Her focus was one hundred percent dialed in on getting to Charlie.

It took almost 40 minutes, but with help from Casey, Blair was eventually able to coax it out of Charlie. Apparently a teacher, a substitute teacher who had been in charge of Charlie's class that day, a teacher who had not been informed of events such as the death of a pupil's mother, had asked the children to write a letter to their mother's as an exercise in handwriting and literacy. The letter was meant to express their love and appreciation for their mothers.

When the teacher came around and saw Charlie's pinched face and blank page she had apparently questioned him on the status of the letter, at which point Charlie said that he ran from the classroom and hid in the little boy's washroom until, mercifully, the final bell of the day rang about 10 minutes later.

Mac watched Alice pace the small space of the bedroom, fuming and sputtering on about how irresponsible the school had been and did Mac know how much they paid in fees for their children to go to that school? *And all for this shit!* She was only silenced when Charlie uttered five heart-breaking words.

"When is she coming home?" he asked, and though it was a mumble, no words had ever been clearer. His eyes looked to Casey who looked to Blair who looked back and forth between each of the twins.

Mac exhaled. How was Blair supposed to answer that? It was an impossible question with a million answers, none of which would ease the broken-hearted boy's pain.

A sniffle from behind told Mac that Meredith had made the journey up the stairs, but when he turned to confirm his suspicion he was surprised to find Dr. Peter Cassidy standing alongside her.

Everyone was there. Except Benny.

Blair took both of Charlie's hands first and held them. He looked at the little boy with such sincere sympathy and love that it didn't seem possible they had only met a few weeks ago and that such a bond had already sprouted. Then with one hand he reached for Casey's hand and looked at her in exactly the same way.

Everyone was silent. He had all of their attention. What would he say? What could he possibly say?

"You two are so dearly loved by everyone around you, you know that, right?"

The twins nodded and his eyes softened.

"And I wish I had an answer for you, but I don't. There's only one person who can explain this to you, and even then I'm not sure it will make all that much sense. But I'll speak to him for you, okay? I'll ask him to tell you as much as he can."

The twins nodded and Mac felt that through their tear-blurred eyes they half-understood what he was saying and were half relying on a miracle, on something to erase the other half of themselves that told them their mother gone forever.

Later that night, after the twins had clamed down, eaten dinner and gotten ready for bed, Benny sat them down and explained, once again, the most excruciating fact of their lives.

While the twins cried and repeatedly asked where their mom was Alice paced the room. "I'm here," she'd say. "I'm right here!" But it didn't matter; she might as well have said nothing at all. Nobody could hear her.

***

After Benny put the twins to bed Alice wouldn't

leave their bedroom and it felt wrong to leave her alone in there, so Mac stayed. He told the others that he had it under control and that she probably just needed some time.

"Don't you think she might want to be alone with them?" Meredith asked.

"I'm not going to bother her. I'm just going to be here. Just in case."

"Let us know if anything interesting happens." Jeremiah said, already halfway down the stairs. Mac winced at how crass his brother sounded and the fact that he knew Jeremiah couldn't care less about how the comment came across. And to make it even worse, Mac knew there was nothing he could do about it. He needed to keep Jeremiah happy, which unfortunately meant allowing him to get away with things he usually wouldn't let slide.

Once the others had left Mac turned back to Alice. She sat cross-legged between the two beds with one arm reaching up and resting on each bed. Mac sat in front of her but she didn't open her eyes or even seem to notice. Roo jumped up and made himself comfortable at the foot of Casey's bed.

They had been sitting in silence for a long while when Alice began to sing. Her voice was soft and tender, like a lullaby.

"Raindrops on roses and whiskers on kittens." She paused and gently cleared her throat. Mac

Middle Ground

watched as she kept her eyes closed and continued. *"Bright copper kettles and warm woolen mittens."* She paused again and breathed. *"Brown paper packages tied up with strings. These are a few of my... favourtie things."*

At the last line a second voice joined in with Alice, her eyes popped open at the sound. Mac stared straight back at her. Had she just heard what he had heard? If she had, then she would have distinctly heard Casey sing the final line of the verse in perfect unison with Alice. They both looked from left to right at the twins, both silent and seemingly asleep. But before Mac could say anything Casey slipped out of her bed and padded across to Charlie's. Mac had to quickly hug in his knees in order to avoid her walking though his legs. Of course, she wouldn't have noticed anything, but he would have. And despite how long he had been dead for he had never gotten used to a human so easily being able to drift right through him.

While Roo took the opportunity to stretch out on the now vacant bed, Casey climbed up into Charlie's bed and nestled in next to her brother.

"Keep going." Charlie said. His voice was quiet but the words were clear. He starred at Alice, whose jaw was slack and eyes bulged like he'd never seen them do before.

"Girls in white dresses with blue satin sashes.

Snowflakes that stay on my nose and eyelashes. Silver white winters that melt into spring. These are few of my favorite things." The words sounded high-pitched and miniature coming from such a small person, but still there was no mistaking them. Maybe it was a coincidence or maybe it was something else but either way Casey was singing the same song her mother had been singing, and more than that, she had picked up exactly where her mother had left off.

Mac couldn't believe his ears and sprang to his feet. Roo lifted his head for a moment, only slightly interested in the activity.

"Something interesting is happening!" He ran from the room. "Something very, very interesting is happening! Everyone! Come, quick! Make sure the doc comes too, he won't want to miss this."

When Mac returned to the room all three of them were singing in unison, their voices a mashup of adult, young girl and young boy.

"When the dog bites, when the bee stings, when I'm feeling sad. I simply remember my favorite things and then I don't feel so bad."

By the end of the song Jeremiah, Meredith and even the doctor stood huddled at the door. Mac turned to them, expecting to find the same reaction he and Alice had had. But they said nothing.

"So?" Jeremiah finally said, unimpressed.

"So? So didn't you just hear that?"

"So Alice joined in on their song. Big deal. Next time feel free to keep me out of choir practice." Jeremiah turned to leave.

"They joined me." Alice said quietly. She stared at the carpet, confused, trying to piece it together, trying to figure it out.

"I beg your pardon?" Dr. Cassidy said, his voice raspy. He cleared his throat and repeated himself.

"I said they joined in with me. I was singing that song and *they* joined in with *me*."

"That's impossible."

"Unless it was a coincidence." Meredith said. "Did you used to sing that to them? They might've been trying to self-sooth. Kids do that, I think."

"I sang it to them all the time."

"Well there you go. Mystery solved." Jeremiah said and turned once again to leave.

"No!" Mac said. "I was here. I saw it happen. I heard it. Alice was singing and when she paused for only a few seconds Casey picked it up exactly where Alice had left it. It was too perfect to be a coincidence."

"That's, like, the definition of a coincidence." Jeremiah said.

"He's right." Dr. Cassidy said. "It could be a coincidence, it could be something else. But we don't know. And the fact is we likely never will."

"So that's it?" Mac said. He was so excited, so invigorated by the experience and could feel it all slipping away and being tucked away as something that happened once and might have been extraordinary but also may have been nothing at all. But why did nothing have to be the default?

"What else is there?" Dr. Cassidy said.

Mac looked around the room at the blank faces.

"Well whatever it was, the show's over now." Jeremiah said and pushed past the doctor and Meredith who shuffled out of the room after him without another word.

Roo jumped up on Mac, a paw reaching up to each of his shoulders and licked his face.

CHAPTER 15: DR. PETER CASSIDY
Was It Worth It?

There was something about Blair that intrigued Dr. Peter Cassidy more than any other human he had observed in the house. Since Blair began working as the nanny, the doctor found himself away from his rocking chair more often than not, simply following Blair around the house, observing him undertake the mundane tasks associated with maintaining the home.

In the laundry room he watched Blair fold miniature tee shirts and in the kitchen he watched Blair prepare breakfast, lunch, dinner and sweet treats for the family. He developed a habit of following Blair all over the house as he vacuumed or dusted or simply pottered about, moving from one task to the next. Occasionally Mac, or Alice, or Jeremiah, or Meredith, or sometimes even Roo would catch him watching and question him, and he would mutter something incomprehensible and retreat to his rocking chair until the others busied themselves with something else and remembered to forget him as usual.

Then he'd go find Blair again.

Dr. Peter Cassidy knew what a homosexual

was and he knew it meant something very different in today's world than it had when he had been alive. But all the same he had never met one before. Never met another one, rather.

Dr. Peter Cassidy half-told one person while he was alive. It happened over a few too many drinks as so many mistakes often do. He was feeling comfortable and talkative and like for the first time in his life he could share a real piece of himself, of who he was, with his closet friend whom he had known since childhood. That was his first mistake.

It was a frigid winter night in 1941. The wind was strong and the snow was coming down thick outside while the fire cracked and the whiskey warmed them inside. Dr. Peter Cassidy and Edward sat on either side of the wood burner, each with a glass in hand.

"I'm telling you, Pete." Edward topped up each of their glasses. "It's a beautiful thing. A respectable wage, a wife, a child, and another on the way. What more could an honest man ask for?" He leaned back and rested his feet on the doctor's footstool, their socked feet only an inch or so apart. Dr. Cassidy didn't say anything and sipped his whiskey.

"Oh don't let it get you down, Ol' Pete. You're a real catch. A doctor! A pediatrician, no less! A bachelor! You're a good woman's dream!"

"I'm not so sure about that." It was more of a mumble than anything, but Edward heard it and latched on.

"Well I *am* sure." Edward nodded. It was a simple fact.

Dr. Peter Cassidy should have left it there, but there had been too many drinks and the temptation to share had been too high for too long. "How can you be so sure there's a woman for every man and a man for every woman."

"What kind of question is that? It's god's will that it be that way. Are you saying you'd rather be alone?"

"Not alone, no. But I don't know…" Peter stared into his drink, his voice quiet. "You know…?" He looked up at Edward. Only a moment passed while Edward processed his friend's words but it was more than enough time for the doctor to realize he had made a mistake. He wanted to take it all back. He wanted to gather up the words out of the air, crumple them up, stuff them back inside his mouth and swallow them. He wanted them to go back to the place he had been hiding them all his life and silently vowed to keep his mouth shut forever if somehow Edward hadn't heard him admit to being gay or if somehow he hadn't understood.

But of course Edward had heard and understood him.

"Excuse me?" Edward physically recoiled from Peter, pulling his feet off the shared cushion and crossing his arms into his chest. His face was creased with disgust.

"Nothing." Peter said, jumping to his feet, defensive.

"That is *not* nothing."

"It *is* nothing. It meant nothing. It was the drink. I didn't know what I was saying. You misunderstood. Please, Edward, listen to me. Believe me." Peter said and without thinking he put a hand on his friend's shoulder. It was an action he had done countless times before, but suddenly the touch was received in an entirely new manner.

Edward jolted at the contact, as if the touch had burned him or as if Peter had suddenly become poisonous.

"Are you *in love with me?*" His words were more of an accusation than a question.

"What? No. Edward, you are my dear friend of too many years to count. This is friendship between us and nothing else." It was the truth. But Edward wasn't hearing the doctor anymore, he was in a frenzy.

"And this," Edward said, now pacing, "this is why you've never liked my Candice. Of course not. It all makes sense now. You've never warmed to her, and why would you with such perverse delusions of our friendship swimming around in that sick, sick, head of yours."

"Candice has nothing to do with this. I find her disagreeable because she is sour and angry and, and perpetually sweaty for no apparent medical reason—"

"I'm leaving." Edward pushed his feet into his shoes and snatched his coat off the back of his chair as if every second it remained touching an item in the doctor's home it might become more and more tainted, infected.

"You can't leave now!"

"I most certainly can, and I will!"

Peter hurried to block the door. "Edward, please." His voice turned to pleading. If he couldn't convince him it had been a misunderstanding then he at least needed to convince him not to tell anyone. "I'm begging you. As an old friend. Please. Nobody can know." A silence passed. "Please." The final word was barely audible.

Peter watched his friend's face, hard and unmoving. He was thinking. "I'll keep your secret." Edward finally said and Peter exhaled a breath he hadn't realized he had been holding in. "On one condition."

It was that one condition that led to Peter sitting across from the hateful local perish priest the following day. Edward sat at the doctor's side, but the chairs were fixed a considerable space apart. The doctor wanted to tell them both that it wasn't a disease they could catch. He wasn't contagious. But their judgment was almost suffocating and he understood that they were not open to negotiation.

Edward persuaded Father Jacobs to 'help' his friend provided that Peter be absolutely and completely willing to follow his guidance without question. It was the only way, he said.

Peter agreed. That was his second mistake.

***

In the following weeks Peter became more involved in the church than he had been in his entire life. Every mass, every meeting, every event, every gathering. Peter was there. And though he did it all to protect his secret and maintain his anonymity, he had never felt more visible, more watched. Every time he turned a corner Father Jacobs' beady eyes followed him, every time he casually bumped into Edward his old friend's eyes would narrow and he'd pull Candice a little closer. And with the seething glares she threw his way, Peter was sure Edward had told her. Though if he were honest, she had always glared at him in that way. It made him feel paranoid. In his mind every glance, every whisper, every snicker was about him. During mass he prayed loudly for all to hear.

It was proof that he was a good Christian man.

It was clear to Peter from the beginning that he was now Father Jacobs' puppet. He had so much to lose – his friends, his practice, his life – and he felt foolish for thinking he had anything to gain by being honest. And now he had no choice but to fall in line.

On one particularly hideous occasion after finishing another Sunday mass, Father Jacobs stood at the alter with a list in his hand.

"This is a list of sinners." He said waiving the paper above his head. His face looked red and hot enough to blister. "This notice is not intended to condemn all parishioners, for I know that we have some deeply generous souls amongst us. This list, however, contains the names of those who have neglected to contribute to the collections basket for three consecutive weeks." Peter relaxed. Since his meeting with Edward and Father Jacobs he had been making considerable donations to the collections basket each week in a pitiful attempt to buy contrition.

Father Jacobs read the names like a grocery list and paused after each to allow those sitting nearest the offender to dole out a fair dose of shame. It was painful to watch those who could hardly afford food for their table be humiliated in a place that should have offered community and support and reprieve from material pressures. When Dr.

Peter Cassidy's name was called he was certain he had heard wrong until all the faces around him turned to scowl. He was a doctor for goodness sakes. The woman next to him tutted and without thinking he stood bolt upright from his pew. "I've paid!" He said and his voice echoed off the walls. Every face of the congregation turned to him. "There's been a mistake." His voice faltered under all of the attention. "I've paid."

Father Jacobs' eyes narrowed. "There has been no mistake." He boomed. "I assure you, you have not paid."

The doctor's stomach dropped as he melted back into his seat. His cheeks burned red. He understood that this was how it would be from now on. This was the best-case scenario. He accepted it. And that was his third and final mistake.

It didn't take long for Peter to start to deteriorate under the pressure. First the intense stress ate away at his conscience and then it moved onto his body until after about six months of unrelenting agony both were so corroded and broken down that he simply couldn't stand to carry on.

At his funeral people gathered and said the kinds of things he had scarified so much of himself to have said about him. *He was a good doctor. He was a decent man. He will be missed.*

Was it worth it? That was a question Dr. Peter Cassidy frequently turned over and over in his mind from his rocking chair. For a long time the answer had been yes. Yes of course it had been worth it. It wasn't even a question. Yes was the only answer. He had no choice. When he died he was alone and miserable and practically begging for death, but that didn't matter. What mattered was reputation and Dr. Peter Cassidy had done what needed doing in order to ensure he died with a respectable legacy intact.

The answer had unfailingly been yes, until Dr. Peter Cassidy met Blair.

There was something about the new nanny that fascinated the doctor and made him question the judgment and self-hatred that had been so deeply instilled and encouraged within himself. When he looked at Blair he saw a happy and normal man. A happy, normal, *gay* man. And it changed him.

The answer was no longer yes, but no. It had not been worth it. Not at all.

Seeing Blair had done something to Peter. It had changed something deep inside of him and as he sat in his rocking chair, as he had done countless times before, one thing began to feel distinctly different. He could feel the shame and misery that had been pressing so heavily down on him slowly lifting, and when it was gone what was left was a sensation of unbearable lightness.

Before he could tell the others what was happening, before he could even realize it for himself he felt a faint tingling pass through his body and a kind of healing warmth on his skin. And while everyone else was busy, Dr. Peter Cassidy finally let go.

CHAPTER 16: ALICE
When We Died

Autumn had always been my favourtie time of year. I loved the colours and the slow but sure chilling of the air as September turned to October and then to November. And even though I couldn't actually go outside and experience it, I was still happy to be able to perch myself at the window and watch it go by.

After everything that had happened I felt more and more that I needed time to myself. Time to think. But the result was always mass amounts of frustration. Even after being dead for months, I still felt like I knew nothing. Things that I thought and everyone else in the house thought to be true could in an instant be turned upside down.

I had been singing to Charlie and Casey every night since the night of the incident or the coincidence or whatever you want to call it. I wanted it to happen again. I wanted confirmation that on top of being dead I wasn't also going crazy. But it never happened again. I kept singing anyways. They needed me and I knew that on some level they knew that they had me and that I was there and that I would never leave them.

I'll admit that it took us longer than it probably should have to realize that Dr. Peter Cassidy was gone. He was always so quiet and to himself that not hearing from him felt normal. And since Blair's arrival, not finding him in his rocking chair felt normal too.

"Just go find the nanny. That's where he'll be." Meredith said.

"He has taken a real shine to that one, hasn't he?" Mac said.

"Who wouldn't? Brings a real warmth into this house if you ask me."

"Bet I can find him before you can." Jeremiah said with a tap on my shoe.

"I bet you can." I said, probably not as nicely as I could have. But I wasn't interested in playing his games today. And I didn't need to with Mac ready to jump to it whenever Jeremiah asked.

"I'll take you up on that." Mac said, too eager. I couldn't help but cringe. Why was he trying so hard?

As the two hurried out of the room Jeremiah elbowed his way in front of Mac and called dibs on the upstairs 'territory'.

A few minutes later when both Mac and Jeremiah returned, breathless and perplexed, neither Meredith nor I were ready for what came next.

"He's gone." Jeremiah said, his voice flat.

"Huh?" Meredith said, half word-half grunt.

"He's gone." Mac repeated like an echo.

Meredith and I looked at each other and then back at Mac and Jeremiah. And that was it. The doctor was gone, he had figured it out, cracked the code, moved on to greener pastures. And the rest of us were still trapped, wondering how the hell he had managed to pull the whole thing off.

I knew that it could happen to anyone, or at least I knew the theory that it could happen to anyone. But knowing that it *could happen* and knowing that it actually *had happened* felt like two very different things. I wanted to know more. I wanted answers. And as usual, nobody had any.

"But *how* did it happen?" I said. "Like *how* did he do it?"

"Who knows." Meredith said. "But I guess it proves that it can be done and that we're all here for a reason, doesn't it? It proves there's something more."

"Like what?"

"It proves we all have something to come to terms with. We all have something to work though." Mac said, almost to himself.

I was so sick and tired of hearing those words. I didn't have anything to come to terms with and I definitely didn't have anything to work through!

"I wonder what it was for the doc." Meredith said.

"Impossible to know." Mac said. "He was always so to himself. So...buttoned up, ya know?"

The twins cheered from the kitchen and Jeremiah popped to his feet. "I'm on it." He said and disappeared into the hallway. I would've been happy to go myself, but Jeremiah seemed to enjoy taking responsibility for keeping up with the going-ons of the house and then reporting that information back to the rest of us. And particularly after being so icy earlier I didn't want to take that away from him.

"How long do you think it takes?" Both Mac and Meredith looked at me. "I mean is there a certain amount of time it takes. You know, a quota or something?"

"A quota?" Mac said.

"Yeah, I mean maybe you just have to do your time and then you're done. Like jail."

"Ghost jail?"

"I thought you didn't like to call yourself a ghost?"

Mac half smiled. I'd gotten him. "I don't think it works that way."

"Okay I know." I waved them off. "I was just throwing it out there. It sounded better in my head."

"But however it happens, it takes work, I can tell you that much. You know that frown of his?

Constantly thinking, right? Well that frown has been in place since the day Jeremiah and I arrived. Even before that I bet. When we died and showed up we found him with his face scrunched up exactly the same as it was yesterday and every other day. I'm not joking; Jeremiah wouldn't even go near him. Thought he was angry and scared of him. Of course it didn't take us long to realize he was harmless. But you get my point, right. Lots of work, I bet. Lots."

Mac and Meredith kept nattering, volleying their theories back and forth, but I tuned out.

When we died. The words repeated over and over in my mind. Mac had never before said anything about his death or Jeremiah's death, in fact he had actively avoided the subject, but now it was *when we died.* Now it was a shared death?

"The old man's working late tonight so Blair is staying late. They're making popcorn and are going to watch a movie. They're undecided on the title as of now." Jeremiah plopped onto the couch next to me and scratched Roo's ear. "I'm hoping for Shrek. Good music in that one."

When we died. When we died. When we died. I turned to Jeremiah and stared at the one thing I had spent so much time avoiding. The bruised line across his thin neck peeked out from his sweatshirt. It was red and still looked sore. As everyone threw out their guesses for movies choices I stared and tried to put the pieces together. It was clear what the line was from, but not so clear why. Jeremiah was so young. Why would he want to hurt himself like that? It felt impossible to guess without more information. I let my head fall back onto the couch and was about to close my eyes when I felt the distinct sensation of being watched. I lifted my head and found Mac staring directly at me.

CHAPTER 17: MEREDITH
Lonely

Meredith understood why everyone was so scrambled up by the recent events, but as far as she was concerned nothing had changed for her. She had no plans of leaving the house. Not now or ever.

Meredith knew what waited for her if she ever left and she knew that staying was the better option by far. The truth was that Meredith was afraid. If she left the house and she didn't end up in the same place as Archie, where would she be? Best-case scenario she would be reunited with her Archie, but she knew that the best-case scenario was out of her reach. That's what happens when you marry someone better than you, Meredith thought.

Archie was a good egg. And it's not that Meredith was a bad egg, she was just more of a medium egg. And she always knew that the place medium people like her went wasn't the same place good people like Archie went. And if she couldn't be with Archie she was happy to stay where she was. What more could she ask for, really? She was comfortable, she had knitting needles, she had friends... sort of.

In particularly dull moments Mac had asked

Meredith a little bit about her life. Her Archie. But even then it had only been a few questions. The doctor had never asked a question and of course neither had Jeremiah. She thought maybe it was because they felt they already knew about her and her life because they had lived in the same house and watched her while she was still living. Maybe they figured they knew her and they didn't need to ask. But it was a different thing to ask the questions and hear a person tell you about their life in their own words. To get their personal perspective. Sometimes, often actually, Meredith wished someone would just ask something. Anything.

Alice had only been around a few months so maybe it was understandable. But on the other hand, maybe it wasn't. If anything, she should be the most curious about the others lives since she hadn't been around to see any of them.

Meredith liked her fellow friends, or roommates. She wasn't sure what to call them but at the end of most days, she liked them. It was only every once in a while that she resented the fact that they seemed to brush her off as just another old lady, happy to knit and nothing else. Doesn't even have two thoughts to rub together. Her entire life, all her stories and experiences were erased by the wrinkles on her fingers and face. But it wasn't the years that had changed Meredith, it was the way people responded to her over the years that had changed.

Meredith felt that if she wanted to be included she had to insert herself into the conversation. She had to push and elbow her way in and stand her ground and space as a contributing member of the conversation. She was as sharp as she had ever been, but felt she had nobody to share it with so she knitted and nodded and pretended not to be bothered by it.

She would've liked someone to just chat with. It was part of the reason she had been so excited when Alice arrived. The chats didn't need to be anything special. They could talk about Blair, or some cute thing Roo did, or the fact that she thought the hot buttery popcorn smelled incredible and it was a cruel punishment that they could all smell it but never taste it. She wasn't picky, they could talk about whatever.

The truth was that Meredith was lonely. But even at the end of a bad day it was still enough for her to never want to leave because for Meredith, most of the time, enough was good enough.

CHAPTER 18: JEREMIAH
Why?

It was the time of year when the windows would frost up at the edges overnight and then slightly thaw during the day just to frost again the next night. Blair arrived at his usual early hour and as he walked through the front door with his coat collar flipped up against his neck, a cold wind chased him inside.

Outside it was dark and miserable, the sun still hiding from the day. And although it looked less than inviting out there, Jeremiah wished more than anything else to be able to slip out the door before it closed. He wanted to feel the cold, and then numbness of the cold. He wanted to leave.

Since the doctor's disappearance Jeremiah had, just like everyone else in the house it seemed, been doing a lot more thinking. If it was all true that he needed to come to terms with something then Jeremiah was happy because his work was done. He knew exactly what he needed to come to terms with and was happy to report that he had already done it. Years ago and many times since he had forgiven Mac, and he had meant it, so what more could he do? It was out of his hands. His work was already done.

But still, a nagging pulled and pushed him

through various emotions from curiosity to confusion to sadness to anger and back to the beginning again.

Jeremiah followed Blair into the kitchen and watched him shrug out of his jacket and hang it over the back of a chair before putting the coffee on to brew. It had been easier for Jeremiah to carry on before the doctor had died and the whole idea of moving on to another place was just a theory. But now that it had happened Jeremiah couldn't shake the uneasy feeling that had settled in deep inside his belly. *If the doctor could do it, why couldn't he? Why wasn't it working? Why wasn't he allowed to leave? What was he doing wrong?*

For a long time Jeremiah thought that it was based on good behavior. Of course he did. It was the kind of spectrum that all kids his age trusted and referred to. Good behavior equaled good, fair results. And bad behavior equaled poor, yet equally fair results. It was only fair.

But what if he wasn't doing anything wrong, he thought to himself. He had done everything he possibly could to escape and he was still trapped in that house which meant that it must be out of his control. It must be someone else's fault.

Jeremiah clenched his jaw. *Mac.* It was the only explanation. It must've been Mac's fault. Mac was the one who wouldn't accept Jeremiah's forgiveness. Mac was the reason Jeremiah couldn't leave.

CHAPTER 19: ALICE
All I Want For Christmas

I always thought that being busy was what made time go by fast. The busier the schedule the less time you had to notice the days melting away and into each other. I would have guessed that time would go by slower now that I was dead and I didn't have all the regular life-things to distract me. But actually, it seemed to be the opposite. My concept of time was now regulated by the small calendar in the kitchen and the changing of seasons outside of the window.

The day I died felt so clear to me in my memory. Then the funeral. Then Blair starting. Everything felt so recent. But the truth was that months had passed and now the days were turning dark by 5pm, snow was falling regularly and the light jackets and sneakers that used to be piled up by the door had turned to boots, puffy parkas and soggy mittens.

The 1st of December fell on a cold, bright Friday. I watched as Blair and the twins burst through the door after the final school pick-up of the week. Fridays were always an exciting day, but I knew this one would be a particularly exciting day. After baking cookies and finishing the laundry, Blair had taken the time to haul the boxes of Christmas decorations out of storage and piled them up in the living room. When Casey and Charlie found them they went into a frenzy, tearing boxes open one after the other. They loved Christmas.

And though I was happy to see them so excited, a pang struck me in the chest. It would be their first Christmas without me. *Would they miss me?* I couldn't stop the thought from creeping into my mind. Of course they would, I told myself. Of course they would miss me. Of course.

I could feel Meredith watching me watch the twins dive into the boxes, unearthing bobbles and bits of traditions I had set only a few years earlier. It always seemed like she wanted to say something but whenever I would turn to look at her, expecting words, she would turn her attention back to her needles and pretend her focus had been there all along.

I glanced at the rocking chair in the corner, half expecting to see the doctor folded up and mulling over whatever it was he mulled. But of course he wasn't there. And although I knew he was gone, it was something I had caught myself doing more than a few times. Even though we never talked much, there was something comforting about him being there, silent or otherwise.

I left Blair and the twins with their decorating project to find Mac, hoping I wouldn't stumble upon Jeremiah first. Shortly after the doctor had disappeared something in the kid had changed. While he had always been a little sharp, his usual saltiness seemed to have turned sour and something sullen and angry seemed to have taken his place. He spent more time alone than I had ever known him to and was uninterested in keeping up with whatever was going on in the house. He seemed to have adopted the 'piece of crap' basement as his own makeshift gym, constantly jumping from pushups to sit-ups to lunges and so on. One time he asked me to join him and I had to stop myself from laughing when I realized he wasn't joking. I couldn't be bothered to do those kinds of things when I was alive and they would've actually benefitted me. No way would I have been convinced to do them now.

Mac felt like my only friend in the house. I knew there were things he wasn't telling me, but it was none of my business and we both knew that if he wanted me to know something he would tell me. So I didn't ask and we talked about everything else. And for the time being at least, it seemed to work for us.

I found Mac in the kitchen bent over a tray of cooling gingerbread. I watched him inhale a few times before interrupting his moment with the cookies.

"Smell good, don't they."

"Incredible." Mac stood up straight but kept his eyes on the rack. "Just a crumb would be enough. Just a teeny tiny crumb and I'd be good. I'm not greedy, just a crumb."

"The whole tray wouldn't be enough for me."

Mac laughed. "You're probably right."

I leaned my elbows on the counter and took a deep inhale. "Gingerbread wasn't even my choice Christmas cookie, but for some reason nothing in the world looks more appealing to me than these things." I inhaled again. "So weird."

"My mom used to make shortbread with a piece of chopped up candied cherry on the top." Mac smiled. "And she would only make them at Christmas. I asked her once if I could have them on my birthday instead of a cake and I remember she paused and I thought I had almost convinced her but then she said no." He paused and bit his lip, his eyes lost in a memory. "Nowhere to put the candles she told me."

"You don't talk about your parents much." I smiled. "It's nice." I realized that the way I said it made it sound like it had happened before, but the truth was I had *never* heard him talk about his parents. Ever. He looked at me and held my eyes for a moment. I could tell he wanted to keep talking about them, but something held him back. He exhaled and looked back down at the cookies.

"It was a million years ago."

Roo jumped up and placed his paws on the counter. He panted, probably wondering what we were so interested in. "Surly he can smell these."

"Oh I'm sure he can." Mac said and patted his pal's head. "What's going on in there." Mac nodded to the living room. "I take it the kids have found the boxes."

"Oh they've found them. I'd be surprised if there was a single box left in there that hasn't been ripped apart and looted for all it's worth."

Mac laughed. "Good for them." He said and smiled.

***

By the time Benny got home the house had been dipped in Christmas and emerged glittering and merry. And it wasn't just the living room. It was every room. The bannister had been twirled with garland and lights and glass icicles hung from the ceiling in the kitchen. Festive figurines and cinnamon scented candles were placed on tables and all available ledges. In the living room the Christmas tree stood tall and blazed with every possible color. It looked like a finger-painted collage of Christmas. I circled the tree and was half-surprised to discover I knew where every single ornament had come from. Some I had bought myself, others were gifts and a few were handmade by the twins.

My eye caught on one particular bauble. It

was a delicate, golden, glittery, circular one with a cream ribbon tied in a bow around the middle. And on the ribbon in soft silver script were the words *All I want for Christmas is you.* It had been a gift from Benny the year before.

I could feel Mac's eyes on me from the couch and figured Meredith was probably watching too. I was about to reach out to touch it when Casey and Charlie came bursting into the room, each pulling one of Benny's arms.

"Look at it!" Charlie said.

"Isn't it pretty! Do you like it, Daddy?" Casey said, hopping by his side.

He still had his coat on and his shoulders were dusted with fresh snow. His navy blue tie peeked out and his brief case was still hanging from one hand. He looked so handsome to me in that moment as he stood looking at the tree and because I stood next to it, it almost felt as though he was looking at me.

"It's amazing." His eyes scanned from one color to the next. "Did you do this all by yourselves?" The twins giggled and looked behind them. Blair held his hands up.

"I didn't do a thing." He said and smiled.

"Well I'm very impressed." Benny said and smiled down at the twins.

"Okay you've shown your dad. Now will you

please wash your hands? Dinner will be ready in two ticks." Blair said and headed back to the kitchen. The twins hurried after him to wash their hands, but Benny stayed.

He walked into the room, right up to the tree and found the same ornament I'd been looking at like he knew where it was all along. He gently lifted it and brushed his thumb over the words. He pressed his lips together and let the bauble fall back to its hanging position and walked out of the room. I watched the ornament sway back and forth a few times before becoming entirely still.

This time when I looked at Mac and Meredith neither tried to look away as if they hadn't been watching all along.

"You okay?" Mac said and I caught something in his eyes I had seen before. Concern. He wouldn't say it out loud, wouldn't bring it up until I did. But I knew he was watching me and wondering how I would react. He was always watching.

"I'm okay." I said and walked over to join Meredith on the couch. Roo jumped up next to me and put his head on my lap.

"It's okay to miss him, you know." Meredith said. I nodded.

"And he misses you, too." Mac said and I looked up at him. He nodded. I looked to Meredith and she nodded, too.

CHAPTER 20: MAC
Nothing But Hope

Alice was upstairs preforming her nighttime ritual of singing to the twins as they drifted to sleep, and somewhat surprisingly this time Meredith had joined her. Not to sing but just to watch. And since Jeremiah spent most of his time in the basement these days Mac expected to find the living room empty, except maybe for Roo who might be sprawled out on the couch, reveling in its vacancy.

Mac stopped short at the door when he saw Jeremiah sitting cross-legged in the glow of the Christmas tree. He leaned against the wall, pressed his lips together and watched his little brother. Mac thought he looked so small, so childlike and curious as he stared up at the massive fluffy pine.

Mac had more guilt and regret than anyone else in the house by a long shot. A very long shot. His guilt was something he tried to address every day but never with the intention of solving it or making it go away because his kind of guilt was the worst kind of guilt. It was punishment guilt and he deserved it.

Though Mac had died too early to learn it, many thought it wasn't his fault. They thought that the blame had been laid a bit too heavy on his young shoulders and that people should've gone a bit easier on him. But even if he had been around to hear these words, he wouldn't have accepted them. And neither would his parents.

Jeremiah stirred from his cross-legged position and Mac pulled himself away from the wall, afraid Jeremiah would realize he was being watched and not be happy about it. But Jeremiah didn't turn around. He pulled his knees into his chest and rested his chin on them for a few moments before dipping his chin in to his chest. Mac watched his brother pull his legs in tighter, closer to his chest. Even under the sweatshirt, Mac could see how tense his little arms and shoulders were. Then, ever so slightly, Jeremiah started shaking. Sniffling. Crying. He kept his head curled in and all Mac could see was a quivering ball of a little boy.

He wanted to hurry over to his little brother and hug him and ask him what was wrong. But how could he do that? He knew exactly what the problem was and the problem was him. It was a truth too real for Mac to look directly in the face so he distracted himself with a common daydream: Jeremiah today, but alive instead of dead.

An interesting fact about Jeremiah is that he was born on Christmas day 1941. Had he still been alive he would've been just about 74 years old. And though Mac almost never allowed himself to wonder at what his own life might have been like had he lived, he often found himself conjuring up ideas of what his little brother's might have consisted of.

The little boy he saw before himself now was certainly scrawny, there was no way around that, but Mac had never met a more determined person, let alone kid, in his entire life. He had no doubt in his mind that had Jeremiah lived he would have broken weight-lifting records and set impossibly untouchable new ones. Who would Arnold Schwarzenegger have been had Jeremiah Tullbridge been on the scene? Jeremiah would've been famous. He would've been someone people talked about. He would've stopped idolizing the greats of his day and become the idolized.

And on top of the success there would've been a family. A perfect family. Children and a wife and a nice home to live in paid for by muscles and an unprecedented work ethic. At 74 Jeremiah would've been happy and fulfilled, satisfied. It would've been a good life.

The thought was almost comforting to Mac until he reached the end and realized it was all a fiction, crafted out of nothing but hope and assumption.

Jeremiah stopped shaking and his small head peeked up at the tree. Mac knew he couldn't contribute anything to the moment so he gave Jeremiah his privacy. It was the only valuable thing he could offer.

CHAPTER 21: ALICE
Too Soon

Blair's husband, Charles, was a surgeon. He worked a long, grueling schedule, which on the one hand was a good thing because it was pretty much the only reason Blair was available to nanny Charlie and Casey. On the other hand though, I knew it meant that Blair didn't always get to see as much of his husband as he would like to.

But with the holidays approaching quickly Blair had been buzzing. They had a vacation booked. A tropical vacation. *10 whole days on sunny, sandy beach chairs!* Blair would say to anyone who asked, or even didn't ask for that matter. He told the twins and Benny. He told the mailman and any person who happened to call the house. His excitement might have been annoying if it hadn't been so infectious. He had the kind of smile that made you involuntarily smile just by looking at it. And his happiness immediately made me happy even though I wasn't the one going on vacation with my husband and I didn't particularly feel I had much to be so happy about.

It was the day before his vacation and we all watched as Blair hummed around the house, making sure everything was in order for the time he would be away. Just watching him made me tired. He had pre-made a variety of meals and stacked them in neat, labeled containers in the freezer and left a list on the counter for Benny to reference for cooking temperatures and times. He had scrubbed every inch of the house and folded every bit of laundry. He was a lifesaver in a perfectly starched, paisley button down and even though I still had less than pleasant things to say about Charlotte, I was so massively grateful she had found him.

University had broken up for the term and just as Blair was slipping his arms through his jacket sleeves, Benny walked through the door.

"You're still here?" Benny said and set his brief case down. "I can't remember where but don't you have somewhere to be?"

Blair fastened the buttons on his coat and smirked. "Now now, Benny. No need to be jealous. All that snow is actually pretty if you get to stay inside and don't have to go anywhere near it." he laughed.

"Yeah, yeah." Benny smiled. I knew he was actually happy for Blair to get some time away with his husband, but I was also certain that Benny wished he could go with them. I was always the one insisting we stay home for the holidays, telling him it wouldn't feel like Christmas without snow. And though I knew he didn't agree, he never once argued with me over it.

"Oh also." Blair said. "Did you get that email I sent you…?" His smile was slightly devious.

Benny was flipping through a stack of envelopes. "Yeah." He dropped the mail back on the table.

"Annnnd?"

"And I deleted it." Benny shrugged out of his coat and hooked it over a hanger without looking at Blair.

"What? Why?" Blair slipped a glove on each hand.

"Because I'm just not interested in all that." He stepped out of his shoes.

Blair mimed dangling a piece of mistletoe above his head. "Tis the season you know. People love *love* at this time of year."

"I get it." Benny said. "But I'm just not ready for… all of that right now. Not yet, okay?"

"Okay." Blair said, not pushing it. "Just a little Christmas prezzie for you. But do me a favor and keep the email. The subscription is paid up for the first three months starting from whenever you decide to register. And from what I've heard it's the best of the best when it comes to dating sites."

"Noted."

"Okay I'm off to fetch the kiddies. Back in a tic." Blair said and disappeared into the snowy wonderland he would be escaping the next day.

A dating site? Blair had given Benny a subscription to a dating site? I could feel my body temperature rising, my heart beat quickening. How could he do that to me? It hadn't even been six months since I'd died and Blair was pushing Benny into some other woman's arms. Or some man's arms for all I knew about this so-called 'best of the best' dating site. I was furious! And because Blair wasn't there to take my beating Benny was next in line.

***

I followed him as he padded into the kitchen. I yelled at him, all variations of *how could you do this to me?* and *How can you just forget about me like this?* Of course I knew he couldn't hear a word I said, but it didn't matter. Every single one of those words needed to come out.

As I continued to tell Benny exactly what I thought of Blair, and Blair's dating site, and Benny dating again, Benny munched on a fresh gingersnap cookie and flipped through the open newspaper on the counter. I heard footsteps behind me and knew I now had an audience but of course that didn't stop me. I didn't care who saw this. In fact, I wanted people to see this. I was in the right and I wanted as many people as possible to know it.

I followed Benny, still yelling, over to the catchall junk drawer where he rooted around, found a pen and returned to the paper. He pulled another cookie off the cooling rack and hunched over the crossword, focused. He was entirely oblivious to my ranting but it didn't matter, I felt like I was making progress and working it out of my system.

I know I would have kept going if Mac hadn't stepped in and tried to calm me down. I felt his hands on my shoulders first, they were gentle but I was electric and jumped at his touch.

"What!?" I said, huffing, furious.

"Okay." Mac held his hands up, palms to me. He meant no harm. "It's okay. Just, take a breather."

"Did you hear what happened?"

"I certainly did." Mac said, not joking at all. "And you have every right to be upset. I agree with you. It's probably too soon."

It was what I needed to hear. Someone agreed with me. It was too soon for him to date. For him to find a new me. It was too soon for me to be forgotten about. My shoulders slumped forwards and I suddenly felt exhausted. "Thank you." My words were half words, half whispers.

I left Benny to his cookies and crossword puzzle and walked to the living room. My arms hung limp at my side and Roo licked my fingers. As Mac and I walked past the stairs Jeremiah looked up at me. He was perched on the third step from the bottom and his face was coated in something other than anger for the first time in weeks. Was it sympathy? Was it pity? Was there a difference? I couldn't tell.

CHAPTER 22: MAC
Merry Christmas

Jeremiah was distant as usual. When Mac wished him a Happy Birthday he snapped his eyes in his direction and said between gritted teeth, *you'd better not tell anyone.* Meredith already knew it was his birthday and Mac didn't see why Alice knowing was such a big deal, but if Jeremiah didn't want anyone to know it didn't bother him. It was one less thing to think about as far as he was concerned.

Mac thought Jeremiah would be in a better mood because Charlotte was back and the last time she had been in the house he had been boarder-line obsessed with her. And to be fair he did seem to be momentarily lifted by her arrival. But then the moment passed and he resumed his sulking.

Benny was busier than ever with the twins. Since Blair had left on his vacation and the twins had been out of school Benny had been whisking them from one activity to the next. First it was building snowmen and then it was crafts at the table and then it was building a fort and then it was a play date. It was never ending. Mac and the others had never seen Benny so involved in his children's lives before, so desperate to keep them both busy enough to distract them from the fact that no matter how many things they did, one thing was still missing and always would be. And to an extent it worked. After their busy days the twins fell into their beds, practically asleep before they could even utter a quick and quiet goodnight to each other.

And even if the twins hadn't noticed their mother's absence in amongst all the busyness, Alice was still there for them. When they were home she followed them around all through the days and she continued to sing to them every night, and for some reason Meredith continued to join her.

This was usually the only time of day Mac and Jeremiah were left alone together. Recently Jeremiah had been surfacing from the basement around this particular time of day. He would sit in the living room with Mac while the women were upstairs and he would stare. Mac knew that Jeremiah wanted to say something, that he was desperate to get something out, but he also knew his little brother well and knew that Jeremiah was delicate and if he pushed too hard Jeremiah would retreat to the basement again and Mac would never get it out of him.

So Mac was willing to wait. For many nights Mac sat with Roo in the living room while Jeremiah stared. A few times Mac tried to make casual conversation but Jeremiah flat-out ignored it. Apparently he wasn't there for idle chit-chat.

***

Christmas Day was a weird day. It seemed like almost everyone, dead and alive, was just trying to keep it together long enough for the day to pass and a new, normal day to begin. There had been hardly any mention of Alice all day. None of the adults seemed to know how to address it. Were they supposed to address it? Were they supposed to pretend it was normal? Or were they supposed to ignore it and wait for the twins to make the first move?

It happened over Christmas dinner. The twins sat next to each other and opposite them sat Charlotte and her new squeeze, Dale. When Mac first saw Dale he thought he had a very round face and thin, sort of wispy hair arranged into a sad kind of comb over, but also a very kind smile. The kids accepted him immediately. They were still at the age where they could sniff out an ally almost instantly and disregard a disagreeable feature without hesitation.

To their left, at the end of the table sat Benny and to their right at the other end of the table was the fancy Christmas-only five-wick candelabra.

Benny began dishing up mashed potatoes and without even a word between them, both of the twins slipped off their seats. Charlie walked to the cupboard, climbed up to the counter and pulled a clean plate from the shelf while Casey precariously lifted the flaming candle feature from the table.

"Woah, woah! What're you doing there little Missy?" Dale said jumping to his feet and carefully lifting the melting candelabra from Casey's grip.

"Making room for Mommy." she said, matter of fact.

Alice's hands lifted to her mouth, she seemed to be holding her breath. Everyone watched the adults watch each other while they all thought the same thing. What the hell were they supposed to say? What were they supposed to do?

Mac could see it written all over Benny's face. He had told them many times. He had sat them down and poked at the pain until he was sure they both understood. He couldn't do it again. He couldn't have that conversation again today.

And thank god for Charlotte, he would not have to.

"Well that is very nice of you, Casey," she said, jumping right in, not missing beat. "And you too Charlie." She stood from her chair. "Here, let me get her some cutlery. And which napkin do you think she would like?" The three of them huddled over a selection of paper napkins, one featuring a snowman, and another a snowy landscape and another a happy pup in a Santa's hat.

"All of them!" Casey said and Charlie agreed. They picked up a napkin each and placed it on top of the freshly laid plate.

"That's really lovely, kids. I think you're Mom would really like this." The twins beamed up at their Auntie.

"Me too." the voice croaked from the opposite end of the table. Benny's eyes were rimmed in red. "She'd absolutely love it."

Mac looked at Alice. Her hand still pressed against her mouth as if it were glued.

"Merry Christmas, everyone." Dale said and held up his glass to the centre of the table. The rest lifted theirs, even the twins clinked their special fizzy apple juice and chimed in a Merry Christmas and it wasn't sad at all. In fact it was quite the opposite.

Mac turned to his fellow housemates. "Merry Christmas." He said and opened his arms to the group. It was an offering and despite any tensions in the house it was surprisingly received with love. Feet shuffled and for a moment, all four of them, even Jeremiah, and five if you include Roo, joined a giant group hug. They were not alone.

Later when the final light was turned out and the day was official done, the house itself seemed to exhale a sigh of relief.

CHAPTER 23: ALICE
Why Not?

New Year's Eve had never been much of a big deal to me. It wasn't that I disliked it for any reason or that I didn't think the idea of a new year wasn't exciting. It was mostly just that even from a young age I found it difficult to muster up the energy for another big party just days after all the thrill of Christmas.

When Benny and I started dating I was happy to learn I had found someone who felt the same as I did and every New Years since it had been our tradition to order Chinese food and purposely forget to notice the clock creep past midnight.

The first New Year since my passing turned out to be more of the same. Charlotte and Dale were still at the house and had promised the twins they could stay up to watch the countdown with them if they wanted to. And because they were six of course they wanted to stay up until midnight. But also because they were six midnight proved to be somewhat of an impossibility for them and by 11:30pm all four of them were passed out in front of the TV while a camera panned over an outdoor crowd of people vibrating in anticipation of the new year. Casey and Charlie were curled up on a pile of couch cushions scattered on the floor,

Dale's arm was around Charlotte's shoulders and Charlotte's hand was limp in a bag of Flaming Hot Cheetos.

Mac, Meredith, Jeremiah and Roo dotted themselves throughout the living room, claiming available spaces to sit and watch the New Year come in.

"At least they left the TV on for us." Mac said, eyes glued to the screen.

"Does that world look weird to you?" I said. "Like do you recognize it as your world too? The one you grew up in?"

"Yeah." He said and shrugged his shoulders. "I mean people are people aren't they. The clothes change and I mean, technology wasn't even a word people used in my day, but looking at these people it's all the same isn't it. Faces."

Meredith nodded but didn't say anything and Jeremiah pretended not to care about the conversation.

In the kitchen I found the remnants of the Chinese food. Stray noodles stuck to the counter in squiggly patterns and things that used to look crispy had turned soggy. I wanted to clean it all up. I wanted to collect the containers and throw them out. I wanted to put my gloves on and spray and scrub until everything sparkled. I wanted to contribute.

Benny had been in his office since after dinner finished. The next term was about to start in a few days and I knew he probably had a painful amount of papers to get through before then. Every once in a while I'd pop by head though door like I used to do. I knew it was different now, that he had no idea I was still there, still checking in on him, but I did it anyway.

On my last check in before he went to bed I lingered. I watched him finish reading a paper, scribble something on the paper in his perfectly illegible professorial script and flip the page over. He dropped the paper on the top of a small stack and exhaled. This is when I usually would've walked over, asked him how he was doing, rubbed his shoulders, kissed his forehead.

I stayed at the door.

He leaned forward, rested his elbows on the desk and scrubbed his hands up his face and under his glasses. He had been working for hours and needed to go to sleep.

Go to bed, Benny. Just go to bed.

He adjusted his glasses and pulled his laptop from a stack to his left and opened it in front of himself. I could hear the faint clicking of his finger tapping the track pad. He leaned back in his chair and crossed his arms, still staring at the screen. Then he learned forward, face close to the screen, absorbed. What was he looking at? And just as I began walking towards him he looked up at the door, cautious, like he was guilty and convinced that he would be caught. He looked back down at the screen and quickly back up at the door before standing, hurrying over to the door, peeking out left and right, and gently closing it.

I smiled. Now I needed to know what was going on. I followed him back to his desk and stood behind him.

I'm not sure what I was expecting. Porn maybe, but not this. It was the email from Blair with the invitation to sign up for the dating website. In garish hot pink lettering was a button that read 'Click to See Who's Looking For You Right Now!'. Benny clicked and I gasped loud enough I thought even he might have heard it. He didn't.

The page redirected to the browser and loaded a selection of profiles with pictures featuring women doing at least one of the following: Yoga, hugging a dog or idiotically prancing on a beach somewhere. And every single one of them had impossibly white teeth. I considered how long it had been since I had brushed my teeth and then remembered it didn't matter. I absently rubbed my finger across the front of them and felt nothing but smoothness.

It was like online shopping but for a date instead of an appropriate dress to wear to your cousin's wedding in the summer. Benny scrolled down the page for a few seconds before a pop-up informed him he would need to register in order to continue viewing profiles. His mouse hovered over the register button for a good while and I was sure he would click it. Why not? I mean he'd come this far. He was going to register. If not tonight then sometime soon. He was alone and it had been his choice to open the email and he was thinking about it.

He closed the laptop. I noted that he didn't close the window first and then the laptop. Just the laptop.

Surprisingly, I didn't feel angry this time and I didn't want to scream at him. As he stood from his desk, flipped off the light and left me standing alone in the dark I felt sad. Left behind.

One of the worst parts of all of this was that I felt like I didn't have anyone to talk to about it. I knew Mac had always been there for me and if I brought it up with him I knew he would do his best to help me work through it, but it wasn't the same. I wanted to talk to someone who could feel what I was feeling. Someone who could empathize with my situation and tell me to either be angry about it or get over it. I couldn't tell which was the sensible option.

It still felt like not enough time had gone by and it was too soon for him to be considering "Becca" in the tiny bikini in Cancun. But of course,

I would feel that way. I was his wife. Or I had been his wife. Would I ever be okay with him dating someone new?

There was only one person I could ask.

CHAPTER 24: MEREDITH
We Can Get By

Meredith was surprised when Alice came to her for advice, but she also understood where she was coming from. Meredith was the only one in the house who'd been committed and married to another human being. And though she knew Alice had approached her due to some kind of process of elimination, she was still thrilled to have been chosen. She even put her needles down for the conversation, tucking them under her left leg to pin the yarn and prevent it from unraveling.

"Am I being irrational? I mean I guess he has to move on eventually, doesn't he?" Alice said. "I don't know, I just don't think dating is a good thing for him right now." It was clear to Meredith exactly what Alice wanted her to say, but she took her time answering. She had an opportunity to make a real friend here and she didn't want to mess it up by spitting out some easy, hasty response.

Meredith truly didn't think Benny wanted to date again. Or at least not yet anyways. She figured he was just trying to get his footing. Alice had been gone for almost half a year now and she bet that his life hadn't felt so good with her gone.

And it's not that he thought it would feel better if he dated. But maybe it would feel different. And maybe different would feel better than the way he had been feeling. Meredith wasn't convinced that Benny wanted to date because he was actually interested in meeting another woman, she figured he wanted to date because he was interested in forcing himself into feeling something other than the hell he was feeling and had been feeling since his wife died.

But how was she supposed to say that to Alice? She knew she only had one chance so she decided to disguise the answer in an anecdote and let Alice connect the dots.

"You know how you always hear people saying that if they were the one to die first they hope their partner finds love again?"

"I know, I know." Alice covered her face with her hands. "I know I should want that for—"

"Well I've never believed them. Not a single one of them."

Alice was silent.

"I loved my Archie so much that the mere thought of him with another woman, even if she was lovely and even if I was dead, is enough to make me want to kill him. You with me?" Alice was with her. She nodded and waited for Meredith to continue.

"Archie was mine and I was his and that was the end of it for both of us."

"So you're saying Benny should never date again?"

"Well the thing is, men are funny things, Alice. They're not like us. Women are made of different stuff, ya know. Stronger stuff."

"Hey." Jeremiah said from the opposite side of the living room. Meredith rolled her eyes. Of course, this would be the moment he would want to add his two cents.

"Not that way. Not muscles. Though we could if we wanted to, mark my words." She pointed her finger at Jeremiah who scowled. She turned back to Alice. "I'm talking about this." She held her fist over her chest, over her heart. "These things are stronger in us. We can get by. But men...." Meredith paused, shook her head and started up again with a new angle. "I don't think he's trying to replace you or forget about you. I think he's just trying to get by."

Meredith watched as Alice sat silent, chewed her lip and processed the words. She wondered if Alice would believe them and if she had made any sense at all to her. Beside her thigh Meredith crossed her middle finger over her index without thinking. Please.

"I think I know what you mean." Alice said. Meredith smiled and waited. She knew there was more coming. "I don't like it, but I think I get it."

Meredith chuckled. "I don't like it either."

"What about you? What if you had died at my age? Would you be okay with Archie finding someone new?"

"Absolutely not. Never. "Meredith paused. "But I hope that somehow I'd be able to get over myself long enough to consider his happiness. I mean, it's really the least I could do for the love of my life." Meredith smiled. "Plus, he'd need someone around just to point out his left shoe from his right." She smiled again and laughed.

Meredith saw the corners of Alice's mouth lift just slightly. It was a smile. A tiny, tiny one. But she didn't care how big it was. It was something. It was hers. She would take it.

CHAPTER 25: JEREMIAH
Never Got The Chance

Jeremiah stopped hiding in the basement when Blair returned from his vacation. He was still angry and still uninterested in talking to anyone else, but he had always liked Blair and found him a nice distraction from the increasingly bitter resentment brewing up inside of him. He had tried to talk to Mac on a number of occasions but somehow the words just wouldn't come out. So he glared. It seemed to be all he was capable of doing lately.

Blair brought presents home from Mexico for the family. Chocolate for the twins and tequila with a worm sunk to the bottom of the bottle for Benny. Jeremiah stared at the bottle for minutes, waiting for the worm to move even though he knew it was dead.

On his first day back, Blair seemed to go into a kind of frenzy and Jeremiah watched him move around the house with the duster in one hand and pulling the vacuum with the other. By the time he left to pick up the twins form their first day back at school, every speck of Christmas glitter had been packed away in boxes and the house smelled faintly of lemon and fresh laundry.

When Benny walked in the door from work

the twins were building a precarious Lego superstructure and Blair was cooking some kind of tomato-ey kind of thing.

"Smells great in here." Benny said as he walked into the kitchen.

"Ratatouie." Blair said and checked a bubbling casserole dish in the oven, a kitchen towel thrown over his shoulder.

"And what're you guys building?" Benny walked over to the table Charlie and Casey were perched at and kissed each of their heads.

"Nothing that will last." Jeremiah said under his breath. For Jeremiah, one of the perks of being dead, or maybe the *only* perk of being dead, was that he could spit out snarky commentary without receiving any stern side-glances from his parents. He could still remember the way his mom used to clear her throat before the stare, as if to say here it comes and don't you dare miss it. And if he did dare miss it and ignored his mother's warning, his dad would step in, always a tad more forcefully with a fist on the kitchen table and a tight *Jeremiah* spit out between pinched lips, his eyes like a frog, bulging, practically spilling out of his head.

His dad had been Jeremiah's biggest support. He was a beefy man and Jeremiah knew how scrawny he must've seemed compared to him. And sure, he was just a kid, bound to grow into something more developed, more substantial, but he knew his dad appreciated Jeremiah's pro-active approach. The weight lifting equipment had been a combined birthday/Christmas present the year before he had died. It was the most extravagant thing Jeremiah had ever received. Actually, it was probably the most extravagant thing anyone in the house had ever received. He thought it might have even been more expensive than his mother's wedding ring. Maybe.

But car sales had been good that year and his dad had said it was all about planting seeds to reap the rewards of growth. The pressure of that comment had almost weighed as heavy on Jeremiah as the weights themselves.

"Can I talk to you for a sec?" Benny said to Blair out of the corner of his mouth. "Just for a second."

"Of course. Give me two shakes." Blair pushed the dish back in the oven, slipped the oven mitts off his hands and followed Benny out of the kitchen. The twins didn't seem to notice, or care. Jeremiah couldn't tell which.

"What's up?" Blair said in the hallway. "Everything okay?"

"Oh yeah, yeah. Everything's good. Well, fine. Everything's fine. You know." Blair watched Benny trip over his words and waited for him to finally get to what he wanted to say. Jeremiah waited too, arms crossed and frowning. "Well the thing is... I mean, would it be possible to—"

"I'm sorry Benny but I really need to get back to the kitchen. What's going on? Are you sure everything's okay?" Even though Blair was hustling Benny his voice was still laced with care and concern.

"I opened that link you sent me."

Blair smiled. "You opened the link."

"Yeah, I opened the link and now it wants me to set up a profile and to be honest I have no idea how to even begin to go about all this and I was wondering if you'd be able to... Well I actually don't even know if you know how to go about these things either but I could just use a bit of a hand with it because I really have no idea and—"

"Say no more, Benny." Blair said with a hand to his shoulder. "I'm happy to help." He patted the shoulder, smiled and turned back to the kitchen.

Jeremiah watched Benny continue to stand in the hallway. Was he sweating? He looked nervous. He leaned closer to listen for breath and found Benny was inhaling sharply, holding it and exhaling long and slow. His eyes were moving fast in all directions as if he were thinking too quickly to keep up.

The thought came to Jeremiah almost immediately: Alice would hate this. Jeremiah stood back from Benny, a smile stretched across his lips. This would be good he thought to himself. It would definitely stir up something in the house.

This could be fun.

Blair stayed late that night to help Benny set up his dating profile. He said he didn't mind since his husband was working through the night at the hospital anyways. Jeremiah wanted to know more about Blair's husband but he knew it was unlikely he would ever meet the man because the only way he could would be if he came to the house and what reason would he have to do that?

Still, Jeremiah was curious about him. He knew he was a surgeon, but he didn't know what kind. He wanted to know how long he and Blair had been together and what their lives had looked like before they got together. Was he funny or serious? How did they meet? How old was he? Did they have kids? Want kids?

After Benny put the twins to bed, he and Blair headed to the office. Jeremiah had never seen Alice rush through the twin's nighttime lullaby before, and he figured if he asked her about it she would deny it. But it was clear that she was desperate to see what they were doing, and Jeremiah knew that even though she would never admit it outright, she didn't want to miss any of it.

And Jeremiah didn't want to miss any of it either. He had died right at the age when the thought of dating was just drifting through his mind. It was an entirely foreign concept to him and so it intrigued him. Never mind the fact that the evening's endeavor also involved the Internet, which didn't exist during his lifetime. What even was it? How did it work? Where was this 'net'? And how did it know everything about everything? Was it a book, or were there a bunch of people on the other end of the screen giving you the information you asked for?

Put the two things, dating and Internet together, and the concept was beyond his level of comprehension. No way was he going to sulk in the basement with this sort of thing going on up here. He didn't have to talk to anyone, he told himself, and he could just watch and then leave when it was over.

There had been a girl. Samantha. She lived on the same block as Jeremiah, five doors down and across the street to be exact. She was one and a half years older than him and had bright red long hair and a slightly crooked front tooth. Jeremiah loved that front tooth. That front tooth gave him the smallest hint of a hope that he stood a chance to be hers. After all, she was a goddess and he was...

Well he might not have been much at the time, but had she been willing to just wait for him to become the person he was meant to be, he knew he could be everything she needed.

He sometimes wondered where she was now and what chump had tried to fill his shoes.

Benny sat in his chair behind his desk and Blair

pulled up a stool and perched beside him. Alice kept herself at a distance, slumped in the chair in the corner while Meredith, Mac and Jeremiah watched over Benny and Blair's shoulders.

"Okay where's your picture?"

"I don't need a picture." Benny said.

"What are you talking about, of course you need a picture. How are all those ladies out there going to know what you're working with if you don't put up a picture?" Blair said and everyone nodded. It seemed to make sense. Benny cringed.

"But what if someone I know sees me on here?"

"If it was someone who knew you they wouldn't need a picture to recognize you. Besides, who cares if someone you know sees you? If they see you on here it's because they're on here too."

Benny was silent. He knew Blair was right.

"Listen." Blair continued. "We live in a superficial world, okay. If you have *nothing else* on your profile you must have a picture. Trust me.

"Fine." Benny grumbled and opened a file on the screen and pushed the mouse towards Blair. "Have at it."

Jeremiah watched as boxes containing moments of Benny's life whirled by. He recognized some of the people and some of the places in the house, but most documented Benny life outside of the house – the life that he, nor Mac, nor Meredith had ever seen. There was a tanned Benny in bright blue swim trunks posing on a sandy beach somewhere with palm trees. Jeremiah had never seen a palm tree before. Then it was Benny and Alice with skis strapped to their feet and bobble hats on each of their heads leaning on poles on top of a mountain. Jeremiah had never skied.

And for the first time all night Jeremiah thought it was a good thing Alice sat on the opposite side of the room. At least she wouldn't need to see pictures of herself alive and living her old life. He could tell that she wanted to be in the room, to hear the conversations and supervise, but that she was adamant on not participating if she could help it.

A seemingly endless stream of photographs flipped by depicting more moments Jeremiah had never had. The twins, the wedding day, travel, University graduation, and then it stopped.

"Okay I think you've gone too far back, I don't even look like that anymore." Benny said.

"Oh I know. I found the one we'll use at the beginning, but this is too much fun to pass up." Blair said through a huge smile and continued scrolling back in time.

"This is fun!" Meredith said. She stood to Jeremiah's right and until that moment he had almost forgotten she was there.

It took longer than Jeremiah expected it to.

There were so many tiny, boring details to add in, but finally by the end of it all Benny's online dating profile was live. Benny was happy to have Blair there, plunking away at the keyboard as Benny mumbled out his answers to questions like 'your idea of a perfect date' and 'what are you most passionate about?'.

"Now we wait." Blair said and clasped his hands together, excited.

For the entire evening, Alice hadn't moved from her chair, hadn't even looked in the direction of the others, but Jeremiah had been keeping an eye on her. He knew she was listening more than any of them. She stayed in her chair even after the laptop had been closed, everyone had walked out of the room, and the light had been switched off.

"Pretty cool stuff, isn't it?" Mac said to Jeremiah in the hall. "I mean can you imagine meeting a gal that way?"

"Can't imagine meeting one at all." Jeremiah said, his voice flat. "Never got the chance."

CHAPTER 26: MAC
I'll Never Tell

Weeks passed but Jeremiah's comment stuck with Mac. *Never got the chance.*

Since the night Benny and Blair had set up the profile there had been little to no progress in terms of the online dating situation. There had been so much excitement around the whole thing and then... nothing. Blair kept telling Benny to spend some time 'browsing' through the profiles. To send some messages to any ladies who caught his eye. But if Benny sent even one message, nobody in the house knew about it and nothing ever came of it except a smug kind of smile on Alice's lips that seemed to grow with each passing day.

Mac wanted to tell Alice that it was okay for her to feel the way she was feeling, that it was okay to feel like she had won and that everyone would understand where she was coming from, but he knew she would pretend like she didn't know what he was talking about so he didn't bring it up.

Never got the chance. No matter where Mac's mind wandered to or how long it was gone for it always seemed to come back to those words. *Never got the chance.*

It wasn't exactly news to Mac that Jeremiah had been robbed of certain experiences when his life was cut short, but it also wasn't something he liked to acknowledge often and while having those words pulse through his brain he found no reprieve from the truth.

Mac had had a taste of dating. He had one girlfriend for 7 weeks called Charlene who everyone described as cute as a button. And she was.

Never got the chance. Mac knew those words were more than a lost experience. They were a warning. He knew that it was only a matter of time before Jeremiah blew and that when he did he wouldn't be able to control how or what happened. Mac had seen it coming, seen it building up since the doctor disappeared months ago and frankly, he was surprised it hadn't happened yet.

Mac wasn't sure what Jeremiah blowing up would look like. Would it be in front of everyone? Would it be to his face? Would he go behind his back and tell everyone the one thing he had tried so hard to keep a secret and then watch as everyone exiled and ignored him and hated him.

It was something Mac knew he couldn't run away from. He wished he were alive again just to have to privilege to flee, to run away and let everyone cool off. But of course, he was dead and confined to the house. There would be no place to hide.

Mac knew that Alice was on to him. She had been prodding him for details more and more lately. He guessed she thought her approach was subtle, but he saw right through it and chose to ignore it until one day she finally forced him to address it.

It was about mid-day, the twins were at school, Benny was at work and Blair was busy cleaning upstairs. Mac was stretched out of the couch, star gazing at the speckled ceiling, trying to create patterns from within the random dots and Meredith sat knitting in the chair.

Mac thought he had almost found the big dipper of foam dots when he absently reached his hand down to the floor beside him and found nothing but hardwood in the space usually occupied by Roo. He craned his neck around to check, expecting to find golden fluff either a little higher or a little lower than where his hand had landed, but the dog was nowhere to be seen, he wasn't even in the room.

Mac sat up and swung his legs to the floor.

"Where's Roo?" He said, his voice slightly more panicked than he had expected it to be.

"Hmm?" Meredith said, pulled from her own thoughts.

"Where's Roo? He's usually right here." Mac pointed to the empty space next to his feet. For decades, Roo had rarely left his side.

Mac stood and paced the room, irrationally checking places he had never seen Roo snooze in before. Was it possible for a dog to pass on like the doctor had? Mac tried to push the thought down. It had never occurred to him before. Why would it? He suddenly felt embarrassed. He had always thought Roo's presence in this afterlife had been for him. A small comfort. But if Roo was gone... And with the timing of everything... Mac would have no one... not even his dog.

Mac hurried out of the room. He didn't want to believe it, but a part of him couldn't help but wonder. He checked all the rooms upstairs. Nothing but Blair changing the sheets on the Charlie's bed. He checked the piece of crap basement and was chased out by Jeremiah who was mid-workout and wanted to be left alone, *please!*

And lastly, he checked the kitchen and immediately wished it had been his first stop. In the center of the floor Roo laid on his back next to Alice who sat cross-legged next to him scratching his belly.

Mac exhaled and rolled his eyes at himself. Had he really believed that a dog could cross over the same way the doctor had? Yes. He had to admit that for a second, or perhaps a few seconds, the whole things seemed entirely plausible. Ridiculous, yes, but what wasn't ridiculous in this place? What rule couldn't be broken? What exception couldn't be made?

"What are you guys doing in here?" Mac tried to sound casual.

"Waiting for you."

"What?"

"We were waiting for you to come find us." Alice looked up at Mac. "Well, more accurately I was waiting for you to come find Roo. And I gotta say, took you longer than I expected. Though I don't think Roo here is complaining. Extra belly rubs for you!" Alice said and patted his belly.

"You kidnapped my dog? Why'd you kidnap my dog?"

"I think the more appropriate word is 'dognapped'. And yes, I did."

"Well... why?" Mac said, struggling to find his words. Alice was being so blunt and it unnerved him.

"So I could get you alone."

"Why?"

"To ask you a question."

"Okay. Ask."

"How did you and Jeremiah die?"

Mac was silent. The house was silent. It was so silent that the silence seemed to be a sound in and of itself.

"I said, how did you and—"

"I heard you." Mac said.

More silence. Alice's hints had been easy for Mac to ignore, but such direct delivery of a question like that was a little trickier to dodge. So he didn't.

"I'll never tell you." Mac said, equally as frank, and waited for Alice's response. If she wanted honesty he would give it to her. It might not have been the way she was expecting it, but if she wanted him to be blunt, he would be blunt. He would never tell her. It was the truth. "You're my friend, Alice. And I can't risk what will happen if I tell you."

"If I'm your friend you'd tell me. You'd know that I would understand."

"Nope." Mac said, his head shaking side to side, his eyes prickling red, desperate. Please, he said to himself. *Please drop this. Please.*

"It's going to come out eventually."

"Maybe so." Mac pressed his lips together.

Alice stood from her sitting position on the floor and watched Mac. *Please. Please. Please. Don't ask me again.*

Alice didn't say anything and instead just stared at him, daring him to cave. And when he didn't she simply grunted and walked right past him and out of the kitchen as if nothing had happened.

Mac exhaled and felt his shoulders slump forward. Roo flipped over and trotted over to Mac. He licked his fingers and Mac half-smiled.

"At least I'll always have you." He said before quickly adding "Hopefully." He didn't want to jinx it.

CHAPTER 27: MEREDITH
I Only Have Eyes For You

Meredith wasn't sure if it was because Valentine's day had passed with Benny asleep on the sofa while romantic films played non-stop on the TV, or some other reason, but one way or another Benny suddenly had a date on the books.

It was a Friday night, which was always a great night for a first date if you asked Meredith. Everything was in line. Everything was perfect. But still, Benny was nervous.

The twins were at their first sleepover birthday party with some kids they had met at their new Jujitsu class. The lessons had been a Christmas gift from Blair and were designed to help keep the twins distracted and busy. It worked.

"I should cancel. The twins might need me."

"That's what I'm here for." Blair said. "Next."

"Next what?"

"Well you might as well get all your reasons and excuses out now so we can move on to the fun stuff."

"What's the fun stuff?"

"Well, have you thought about what you're

going to wear?"

Benny looked down at himself. "I think this looks good." He said and Meredith couldn't help but snicker from her spot on the bed as Blair tried not to let his eyes bulge too big.

Everyone sat lined up, shoulder to shoulder on the bed with Mac on the right side, Meredith in the middle and Jeremiah on the left. Alice was nowhere to be seen, though Meredith would've bet money she was standing, or pacing probably, just outside the door. There but not there. It seemed to be her position of choice lately.

Blair shook his head no. "Okay you need to ease up a bit. Just relax. This is fun, remember? We need some music." Blair practically skipped over to the speaker and Meredith watched him plug in his phone and apparently select music from the screen.

"How do they do that?" Jeremiah asked no one in particular. "I don't get where it's coming from."

"Me either." Mac said.

The technology was also beyond Meredith but she didn't care to ask questions. She simply took it for what it was and remained thankful to have been alive in the time of the record player.

Almost immediately the music began wafting through the room and Meredith found she was delightfully surprised by Blair's choice. As Benny rooted through the closet and held up different options for Blair to swat away Meredith let herself enjoy the mellow but pleasing blend of jazz and swing and Motown and everything in between. She couldn't help but smile and didn't realize her toes were lightly tapping to the rhythm of each song.

Most of the songs on Blair's playlist were oldie classics sung by newbies. And some of them, Meredith noted, took such a detour from the original that she almost didn't recognize them. But it soon became a game to her, a personal challenge, to recognize the song and note the title and original artist as quickly as possible. The faster the better, of course.

She recognized "Can't Take My Eye's Off Of You" almost immediately and whispered *Frankie Valli and the 4 Seasons* to herself with a self-satisfied grin. But the next one, "Put your head on my Shoulder", took her a little longer to catch on to and she couldn't quite remember who sang it. Paul something, she said to herself. Paul, Paul, Paul.

Meredith was almost relieved when the next song came on. It came with a kind of permission to move on from the last song and try again on the new one. She listened closely. It felt like looking at someone you hadn't seen since childhood. You recognized them, but so much had changed. Then it hit her. It was more modern and more fluffed up than the Frank Sinatra original from 53', but when it got going it was unmistakable. It was her and Archie's song. Not just their wedding song, their everything song. They wore records out listening and dancing to that song alone.

Without realizing, or without caring, Meredith closed her eyes and let herself sing the words.

"*I only have eyes.... For you.*" She sang, choking on the last word. She kept her eyes closed and cleared her throat, ready fort the next line.

She didn't care that Mac and Jeremiah were watching her, staring at her. Even Alice had peeked her face around the corner of the door to see what was going on. It didn't matter. Meredith hadn't heard this song since she'd died and she wasn't going to let something like an audience stop her from enjoying herself while soaking up every last note of it.

That was when the music stopped. Brutally cut off mid *sha-bop sha-bop*. Meredith's eyes popped open faster than anyone had seen her move before and just as fast as they had opened they filled with tears.

Benny had finished dressing. A jacket, a collared shirt, chinos. Meredith thought he looked nice.

She pinched her lips together, knowing everyone was watching her. Waiting for her to do something and probably hoping she wouldn't cry so they would then have to take pity on the sad old lady. She knew what they were thinking. They didn't want to deal with her. She tilted her head down for a moment of privacy and held her breath, trying to block out everything and everyone around her.

She felt a tap on her shoulder.

She opened her eyes and found Mac standing next to her in his blue ruffle tux, his hand extended, palm up to her. Benny and Blair had left. The room was dark except for the streetlight filtering in through the window behind Mac.

"May I?" Mac said and moved his hand slightly closer to Meredith's.

She frowned, not knowing what he meant.

"Please." He said, offering his hand again.

Meredith wiped her wet hand on her old dress and scooted off the bed. She looked behind her and saw Alice at the door smiling, pushing her on.

Mac took her hand and led her into the middle of bedroom.

"What are you doing?"

"I know a little Sinatra." Mac said, in his classically light tone. The one that was able to diffuse the tension of every situation. He guided one of her hands to his shoulder and placed his on her back. He held the other in the air.

The pair began lightly swaying back and forth

and after a few silent moments Mac's voice started up. Quiet but confident. Slower than the song, but still beautiful.

"My love must be a kind of blind love. I can't see anyone but you."

Meredith sniffled and Mac paused and Meredith rested her head on his shoulder. Mac continued.

"And dear, I wonder if you find love. An optical illusion, too? I only have eyes for... you."

Meredith kept her head on Mac's shoulder as he took his time finishing the song. At the end he slowly twirled her and kissed her hand before letting go.

"Thanks for the dance, Doll." He said, his words so quiet Meredith was sure the others hadn't heard. And she liked it that way. She hadn't felt so noticed or so special for years and she wanted to claim every second of it.

"Thank you." She mouthed back to Mac. It was all she had. It was all she could say. She knew that no matter how many words she had or how carefully she picked them she would never be able to express to Mac what he had done for her or what it had meant to her.

Because of how young Mac looked and how not young she knew she looked, Meredith often forgot that they were both born in the 30s, and only four years apart. She wondered what he might've looked like had he been able to see all the years she had seen. Handsome, she thought. A little more hair on his chin and his chest and definitely he would have been handsome.

For that one dance with her eyes closed Meredith felt like she had her Archie back. He was all she ever needed. When they were young, the plan had been to have their own babies. And when they learned that they wouldn't be able to, the plan was to adopt babies. But in the end time crept by and they couldn't get the paperwork straight, or maybe the paperwork couldn't get them straight. So no babies came but no love was lost.

People told them both together and separately that it wouldn't last. They said that people don't stay in love with their spouses, that they needed the kids to give them something to talk about and focus on when the romance drifts away. But they were wrong. Of course they were wrong. Kids or no kids, Meredith knew that even forever would never be long enough with him.

As Meredith walked out of the bedroom she couldn't help but smile. She wondered if maybe she had been wrong about this bunch. Maybe she didn't have to be alone. Maybe she had been wrong all this time and had never been alone at all. Not even a little bit.

CHAPTER 28: ALICE
I Don't Want To Be Forgotten

The date was awful. Terrible. Painful, even. And I wasn't ashamed to say I was happy about it. It was what he deserved.

The next morning while drinking his coffee and reading the paper the phone rang. Without looking Benny answered.

"Hello." He said, wiping toast crumbs from the corner of his mouth.

"How was it? Tell me everything!" The voice was loud and grating and entirely unique and unmistakable. His face fell. It was too early in the morning for this, even for Benny.

"Good morning, Charlotte." he grumbled.

"Ah screw the morning, tell me about last night!"

"It was terrible."

"What?"

"Terrrriiiibbbblllleee. Terrible. Never again."

"Well you can't just give up after one try. I mean everyone's got first date horror stories. They're funny. They build character. You gotta get back out there!"

"Goodbye, Charlotte." Benny said and hung up on her in the casual way only siblings can manage.

The conversation couldn't have gone better if I had planned it. I couldn't contain my smile and to be honest I didn't want to. I would've been happy for it break free of my face and fly around the room like an obnoxious parade of my complete and unrelenting joy.

"I can see you're very upset about the outcome of the date."

The voice came from behind me. I hadn't heard Mac come in.

"Oh come on." I said. "I'm allowed to feel a little happy about this."

"There is nothing *little* about all this." Mac said waving his hand in my direction. "I feel like you're about to break out in dance or something."

"What if I did? Would you dance with *me*?" I smirked.

"That was a one time thing." Mac said "You have to be here a long time before you get one of those."

"Fair enough." I couldn't help but laugh. "But that was incredibly kind of you. I wish you could've seen it from my perspective. You have no idea how much that meant to her."

"That's what I'm here for. The dancing man in the blue tuxedo. At your service." Mac said in a showy voice. He was downplaying it and I knew he knew it but I didn't want to embarrass him so I didn't push it.

Benny's phone buzzed next to his newspaper. Mac and I watched as he picked it up, stared at the screen and set it back down. He tried to resume reading his paper but couldn't seem to focus.

Instinctively I hurried to the phone to catch the message before it disappeared. It was from Charlotte. *Give it another chance. Everyone should find true love in their life.*

I felt my smug smile drop from my face and almost thought I heard it thud onto the floor. I looked at Mac who had read the message over my shoulder.

"What the hell is that supposed to mean?"

"What?" Mac said. He was playing dumb but I wasn't having it.

"*Everyone should find true love in their life?* What the hell is that supposed to mean? What does she think I was?"

"I don't think that's what she meant—"

"She's happy I'm dead, isn't she! She was just waiting for me to drop dead so her brother, her poor brother could finally be free of me and go on to find the real love of his life!"

"Alice, I think you might be—"

"Don't you dare say overreacting!" I said, half knowing I was over reacting.

"I was going to say I think you might be reading into things a little more than you should."

"I gotta go." I said and stormed out of the kitchen. I wanted to be alone but I knew my choices for privacy were limited. Jeremiah had claimed the basement as his own and Meredith was in the living room. I ran up the stairs, taking two at a time.

Mac waited long enough for me to cool down before coming to find me. I wondered how many places he had to look before he finally got it right. As far as I knew, he had never seen me come to this place before.

"An interesting choice." He said as he walked into the master bathroom.

I knew I probably looked ridiculous lying in the empty bathtub, particularly due to my red plaid pjs, but I couldn't have cared less. This tub had been the thing that sold the house to me. It was a huge free standing, claw foot white bath positioned perfectly to look out the window with a view of the hills and if you squinted you could even see the river, or at least try to convince yourself you could see the river in the far, far distance.

"I loved this tub."

"I bet." Mac said. "Looks luxurious. We definitely didn't have this bad boy in here when I was alive, I can tell you that much."

"Care to join me?" I said and squirmed my legs to one side of the tub. There was more than enough room for the two of us. Even Roo could fit if he managed to find us.

Mac stood silent with his hands in his pockets for a moment before shrugging his shoulders and climbing in. "Ah what the heck." He said. "Wouldn't mind taking this bad boy for a spin." Mac extended his legs to the left of mine, his feet rested at my hip and mine at his. He leaned back and draped his arms over the edges of the tub. "That's the stuff." He said.

I couldn't help but laugh. He really did bring a level of cheerfulness to the house that seemed to make everything slightly more bearable.

I leaned my head back on the edge of the tub and closed my eyes. "This was my thing." I said. "A good soak used to be able to fix almost anything."

"I'll admit, I was more of a shower man myself, but I did occasionally have a bath and I never complained about it if you know what I mean."

"Can you remember what it felt like?"

"What do you mean?"

"Like when you first stepped into the water, just one toe and then your whole foot. And the water would be almost too hot to be comfortable, but anything less wouldn't be hot enough, you know, wouldn't be as satisfying. I used to love that feeling." I looked at Mac who was smiling and nodded.

"For me it was really, really cold winter days."

"Cold days helped you relax? That's literally the opposite of a hot bath."

"No." Mac laughed. "I used to love the feeling of them. There's snow everywhere and the sky is blue and the sun is so, so bright you almost don't want to open your eyes, but you force yourself to because it's so beautiful and so untouched and you know it won't last. And the air is so incredibly freezing cold it feels likes it's actually burning your nose. It's a kind of happiness that hurts."

I nodded. It was all I could do. He knew exactly what I was talking about. A kind of happiness that hurts. That was it.

"I feel like I'm losing that feeling. Like the more time I spend here the more I forget what it used to feel like." I said. "I don't want to lose that."

"It's scary when it starts to melt away, isn't it?"

"I can feel it slipping and I'm not ready to lose it. I'm afraid of what will happen if I do. I don't want to forget what it felt like to be human. I want to remember everything and I want them to remember me." I paused. *Okay, not talking about a hot bath anymore.*

I lifted my neck from the edge of the tub and looked at Mac. "I don't want to be forgotten and I know that sounds selfish and I should be happy that everyone is getting on with the grieving process, but I'm not. It's been eight months and they're doing so well without me. They've had a Christmas without me. Soon the twins will have a birthday without me. They're doing everything without me. Hell, with Blair and his blueberry pancakes every morning they eat a better breakfast than I ever gave them. Everything is happening as it was always meant to happen, just without me. Except it's kind of with me because I'm here and I have to watch them forget about me." I breathed, finally.

"And Benny is a good guy. That first date might not have gone well but it's only a matter of time. With all that online dating stuff he'll be scooped up in no time. And I know I have no right to resent him for wanting that, and I know there are good women out there, but... I don't want to be replaced. I don't want to become the woman who came before the woman who raised the twins and grew old with Benny... Does that make me a monster?"

Mac didn't say anything so I nudged him with my toe. He jumped at the jab and pretended to wake up from a deep sleep. "Sorry. Did you say something?" He said and I rolled my eyes and wedge my toes into his ribs.

"Come on!" I said, trying not to smile. "I just poured my heart out to you and you aren't taking it seriously!"

"That's because it's impossible to take you seriously. Not the bath stuff, that stuff was very serious, but all the stuff after that. *You are their mother, Alice.* They won't forget you. The end."

"Okay." My voice was quiet. "And Benny?"

"Same." He said in his casual tone. "Dead or alive, you're the mother of his children. I think you're safe." Mac draped his arms over the edges of the bath, closed his eyes and leaned his head back. "Now." He said. "Can we please enjoy this bath?"

I pinched my lips together. It made sense the way he said it, so plainly, so simply. But it still didn't change the fact that deep down I'd rather Benny be just a smidge unhappy for the rest of his life than find someone better than me. I figured he could take just a smidge.

I closed my eyes and leaned my head back. I tried to remember what it felt like to float in a tub full of water, weightless. To stay in too long and let my skin prune and my body overheat.

Mac had a real talent for timing. He always seemed to know what to say or do in exactly the moment it needed to be said or done. And that was exactly why I needed to know his secret. It just didn't make sense, I couldn't make it add up. What could he possibly have done in the past that would cancel out all the goodness and kindness pouring out of him now? I knew that nothing could change my opinion of Mac, but still, I needed to know.

CHAPTER 29: JEREMIAH
Only An Accident

On Jeremiah's 7th birthday there had been a new soccer ball, a cheese pizza and a cake which his mother had haphazardly shaped into the number 7. There had also been a Christmas tree in the background but it had been a tradition for the family to always forget about Christmas for just one hour that day and focus all attention on the birthday boy.

All in all, from the fragmented memories he had of the day, Jeremiah thought his 7th birthday had been a pretty great birthday. But no matter how great a day he told himself it had been, it was nothing compared to Casey and Charlie's 7th birthday.

He understood that maybe the party was meant to compensate for their mother's death or hide their mother's death or just be so in your face that you had no choice but to think of something other death, if only temporarily. And to be fair, since it was virtually impossible to focus on anything else, it actually kind of worked.

On the day of the party the house was even more hectic than it had been on the day of the funeral. Thanks to Blair, there were rainbow streamers tied from the ceiling and balloons floating and bunched in every available corner. The walls were plastered in posters and banners wishing the twins a happy birthday and sparkly confetti dusted most tabletops.

And that was just the decoration.

There were so many guests that Jeremiah could hardly move for fear of accidentally walking though one of the dozens of small children racing around the house, high on life and laced with birthday sugar. Jeremiah watched and thought the whole thing was... a lot.

"Jeeze" Jeremiah said, flattening himself against a wall to avoid a small blond, maniac. "When are they all going to leave?"

"They'll drop eventually. This is the height of it." Alice said from the corner. Jeremiah noticed she had hardly moved all day, though he suspected this time it wasn't because she didn't want to participate and more likely that she literally couldn't move. There simply wasn't enough space.

"Well I hope you're right. Any higher than this and their heads will pop off." Jeremiah dodged another frantic small being but tripped backward in the process.

"There's room over here." Alice called over the heads of buzzing bodies. Jeremiah had no choice. He needed a hide-away. He slowly maneuvered his way over to Alice's corner and tucked in next to her. To conserve space, she automatically put her arm around his shoulder and shuffled him closer to her. He usually would have objected to such closeness, but with the confined space, his height compared to hers and the placement of limbs it really just made sense, so he let it slide.

From his new vantage point he could see Meredith and Mac huddled in the opposite corner and almost waved before remembering he was mad at Mac. And he couldn't wave to Meredith because how would Meredith know it was meant for her and how would Mac know it wasn't meant for him. No wave it was.

Jeremiah knew he could have retreated down to the piece-of-crap basement, or even upstairs to one of the bedrooms if he didn't want to be involved in all the hustle of the party. But the truth was that a part of him liked the hustle and he knew he would regret not seeing it. The house could get so dull and parties like this were so rare that he just couldn't resist.

Plus, Charlotte was there.

Though he couldn't quite put his finger on the reason why, there was something about Charlotte he had always liked. He knew that her personality was actually quite grating and he had heard others refer to her an 'acquired taste' but that didn't matter to him. Jeremiah liked her. She was the weird, funky aunt he never had. And not because he had died too early, but just because he had never had an aunt like her.

"I don't even know half of these people." Alice said. Jeremiah looked up at her and saw she was squinting at the crowd and wondered what help that was. They were clearly close enough to see and scrunching up her face wouldn't make her suddenly remember them.

"I recognize some of them, but not many." He said, and before Jeremiah could stop himself he too was doing the eye-scrunch thing as he looked out at the crowd. He recognized Charlotte of course and she had brought Dale with her. Blair was there and he also recognized a few folks from the funeral who's names he didn't know like the blond woman who stood in the corner holding a balloon and a birthday gift bag. She looked about as out of place as he knew he and Alice would have looked had the humans been able to see them crunched into the corner, watching.

"They must be the owners of these mongrels." Jeremiah said as a freckled boy zipped past.

Alice laughed. "You know, you aren't much older than--."

Jeremiah snapped his head up to look at her. He knew what she had meant and he could see that her expression had dropped and that she regretted the way it had come out, but he couldn't resist.

"Oh really?" he said. "You think you know how

old I am?" His words oozed out from between his clenched teeth. "Tell me how old I am, Alice. I'm dying to hear how old you think I really am."

In what was meant to be a gesture of comfort Alice lifted her arm that had been draped around Jeremiah. She meant to reach for his shoulder but her hand landed on his neck, right across his bright red, never-healing scar and within less than a second Jeremiah leapt away from her, entirely unaware and uncaring of who or what he collided with.

"I'm sorry!" I didn't mean to—

"NEVER!" he said. "Don't you *ever* touch me—"

"Jeremiah, I really didn't mean to… I'm so sorry I was just…"

Jeremiah wondered if Mac and Meredith were watching from across the room or if there was too much going on between them for them to notice. He knew it had been an accident but it didn't matter, what could she say now? What could he say now? He turned and ran. This time he didn't try to dodge and ran through multiple people on his path and with each pass through he felt that uncomfortable tightening. Like something gripping him and then releasing. Running through so many people, one after another, the sensation turned into something like a pulse. A grip and a release then another grip and release.

Finally he made it to the stairs. His body tingled and though it wasn't painful, it wasn't pleasant either. In less than one minute he had passed through more humans than he had during his entire time in the afterlife. He perched on a step about half of the way up the stairs and waited for the pins and needles feeling to fade.

On the left side of the bottom three steps was a pile of jackets Jeremiah vaguely remembered dodging on his way up. A small girl with a long frizzy braid was curled up and passed out on top of the jackets, her eyes closed, her mouth hanging slightly open. Jeremiah saluted her. It seemed the party had been too much for her as well.

Jeremiah climbed the rest of the stairs and found himself walking to Benny's study. There was a small bench by the window that overlooked the front door. He liked to sit there every now and again and watch the slightly smaller cars drive by and the slightly smaller people walk around.

And although he was happy to hide alone in the study until the party ended, Jeremiah couldn't help but think of what might be going on downstairs. Specifically what might be going on with the others. And even more specifically, what Alice might be telling them.

Had he over-reacted? He knew it had been an accident, but did that make a difference? Was it automatically forgivable just because it was an accident? And if he wasn't able to forgive her was that his fault or hers? Who's fault was it? Who was to blame? Who would have to deal with the unforgiveable-ness forever?

Mac, he thought, realizing he was no longer thinking about Alice and the stupid scar around his neck.

It was Mac's fault. All of it. He was to blame and he was the one who should have to deal with it.

As Jeremiah sat at the window he completely lost track of time. He didn't notice the screams of play fade and the music turn off. And though he sat staring out the window with his chin resting in his hand it wasn't until he noticed the people leaving the house from the door directly below him that he realized that the sky had darkened impossibly fast, as it only can during unexpected late spring storms. Rain poured from the sky as partygoers rushed to their cars, pulling the small hands of their sugar-caked children behind them.

Fat drops of water hit the window but Jeremiah didn't flinch. His jaw was set tight.

He touched his fingers to the scar at his neck, lightly grazing it before slowly digging his fingers in, pulling as the flesh. He couldn't feel anything but that didn't matter. He would never forget what it felt like. He had taken a big breath before it happened and so he died with that tight feeling of trapped air in his lungs. He remembered feeling like he might burst, if not from the chest then definitely from the throat. The pressure was unimaginable and the seconds were longer than Jeremiah had ever known them to be before.

He remembered thinking it was like playing a game: how long can you hold your breath? All children had done it. If not for victory than for the beautiful feeling of release that came with that first breath after a long hold.

In his last seconds Jeremiah remembered praying for that release, begging for it.

It wasn't supposed to happen like that, after all. It was only an accident.

CHAPTER 30: ALICE
I'm Not Missing This

I was in the kitchen with Blair and Benny when it happened and I would have missed the whole thing if Meredith hadn't hurried in to get me.

Benny had come home from work that day in a particularly good mood, and frankly, it bothered me. He was a little later than usual. Late enough for me to notice the lateness but also not late enough for Blair to be worried and ask where he had been. Thankfully, Blair was nosey and needed to know what had put such a big smile on Benny's face.

Blair was chopping carrots for something bubbling on the stove when Benny walked into the kitchen in sock feet but still dressed in his suit.

"I'm sorry." Blair said and smirked. "Is that... humming I hear? Benny are you humming?"

"What?" Benny said, smiling.

"Humming, that buzzing, music-like sound coming from between your lips."

Benny's eyebrows quickly lifted up in a playful gesture. "So what if I am." He said and took his suit coat off before carefully folding it in half and placing it on one of the kitchen island barstools.

Blair and I watched, amused, as Benny padded over to the cupboard and pulled out a tall glass and then over to the fridge and pulled out a carton of orange juice. He filled the glass almost to the top and drank it all at once.

"Blair had stopped chopping and stood staring at Benny across the island, a small smile pulling at his lips.

"What?" Benny said, licking his lips and looking at the bottom of his now empty glass.

"Where have you been?"

"Work."

"Yeah. And then."

"Just work." Benny said and smiled. I knew that smile. It was his I know you know I'm not saying everything smile and I want you to ask for more. Again, thankfully, Blair was nosey and hardly needed an invitation.

"And what exactly did you do at work today?" Blair said, more than willing to play along in Benny's little game of questions and clues.

"Oh you know. A little teaching, A little marking."

"Mmhmm. Naturally."

"A little coffee." Benny said and paused.

"Coffee?"

"Mhmm. Coffee."

"When?"

"Just an hour ago."

"Hmm."

"What?"

"Nothing."

"Were you alone?"

Benny paused and smirked and I felt my body stiffen.

"How do you do that?"

"Do what?' Blair said, matching Benny's smirk.

And that was when Meredith rushed into the kitchen and told me I needed to come with her. *Now.* I wouldn't have left if it hadn't have been for the look on her face and the speed she come into the kitchen at. She meant business.

She tugged at my arm but my feet stayed glued. Who had Benny been having coffee with? And why had it put him in such a good mood?

"Fine." Meredith said in a huff and hurried out of the kitchen, leaving me planted to my spot. "I'm not missing this."

I watched her disappear around the corner and though I had been so sure I wanted to stay in the kitchen to hear the rest of the conversation I found myself moving towards the door, following Meredith.

She stood at the door to the living room, peeking in but not exactly trying to hide herself. I stood on the opposite side and peeked around the edge of the door. The twins sat on the couch watching a cartoon. They were entirely oblivious to Mac and Jeremiah who stood practically in front of them.

Jeremiah's chest was puffed up and his face red. His jaw was set tightly as if made of stone and as he spat out his words at Mac he bounced up on his tip toes, apparently trying to match Mac's height.

I turned to Meredith who lifted her eyebrows. She was right. I did want to see this. Especially if it was headed where I thought it might be.

"Could we have a little privacy?" Mac said, almost spitting the words at Meredith and me. Until that moment I had almost forgotten we were visible to the two of them and had hardly tried to conceal my presence from them.

"No." Jeremiah said, jabbing Mac on the shoulder. "I'd like them to stay. Why can't they stay, Mac? Are you afraid of what will happen? What they'll find out? Afraid you won't be the favorite anymore?"

"This is between me and you, Jer. That's all."

"Oh don't *Jer* me." Jeremiah's voice was hostile, even for him. "We're all in this together, right? Isn't that what you're always saying? We need to be able to lean on each other. Forever's a long time. These are all your words, Mac."

Mac closed his eyes and we all watched as he took two deep, long breaths. Calming himself. But when he opened his eyes again there was no calm.

And when he turned to look at Meredith and me I was expecting to see anger. But I was wrong. There was no ager. There was pain. Terror. It was clear Jeremiah was going to spill the beans about whatever weighed so heavily on Mac and that Mac felt there would be no recovering from it.

But I knew that no matter what Jeremiah said, no matter what secret he unearthed it wouldn't change my opinion of Mac. It couldn't. I had been dead for almost ten months now and had come to know him as a compassionate, kind, person. A good person. I thought nothing could change that. It was simply impossible. I was wrong.

CHAPTER 31: MAC
Gusts Of Air

Mac knew it would come out eventually, and though he had often wondered how it would happen, in his mind it had never looked quite like this. He tried to comfort himself by saying that at least the doctor wasn't there to witness the charade. But of course it wouldn't have mattered if the doctor had been there because he was the only person other than Jeremiah who knew how the two of them had died. He had seen it happen.

He figured Meredith had probably over the years figured out some of it, half of it maybe. She may have been quiet but he knew she was no fool. Even when her eyes were on her knitting needles, she was watching and if not watching then always listening. He figured she would be surprised by parts of it and maybe she would keep her distance for a while but eventually he thought she might stop judging him and move on. Mac knew he was going to be stuck in this afterlife for a very long time if not forever, and he knew that if anyone else in the house was likely to be there with him it was Meredith.

The worst one would be Alice. He knew she wouldn't take it well. He had killed his little brother, after all. How could she forgive him for that? How could he expect her to?

Mac stood in front of Jeremiah watching everything happen in slow motion.

As Jeremiah's words fired out of his mouth like missiles directed at Mac everything went silent in his head, replaced only by a faint buzzing noise. It felt like an out-of-body experience. Mac wondered how that was possible. He didn't even have a body. How the hell could he feel out of it?

Still in slow motion Mac turned to watch Meredith and Alice ingest the truth. Their jaws slack, their hands covering their mouths, their eyes bulging. It was as if the truth was too much to take in, too big to process and now, any second they might burst.

The strangest part of it all to Mac was the twins sitting on the couch staring blankly through him to the TV at a spread of colorful, dancing animals. How many moments like this had happened before? Moments where nothing was happening for one person and everything was happening for another. Mac figured there must've been quite a few. Things were happening and not happening at the same time all the time.

Mac felt a wetness on his hanging fingers and looked down to find Roo sitting at his feet, looking up at him. A friend. His only friend.

Mac looked back up at Jeremiah whose mouth

was still moving, tears still burning streaks down his cheeks, his finger still pointing and shaking in Mac's direction.

"You aren't even listening to me! Are you?" The words were faint at first.

Mac watched as Jeremiah wound up and kicked at his shin with all his effort. Mac felt the impact, but no pain. Then came Jeremiah's small fists drumming one after the other across his stomach. Impact, but not pain. When Jeremiah looked up at Mac he was panting and seemed to be wishing Mac had felt even one of those blows as much as Mac wished it himself. He watched as Jeremiah's hands fell to his sides and his shoulders slouched.

"You don't even care, do you?" Jeremiah said. And though the words were the quietest Jeremiah had said throughout the whole confrontation Mac heard them louder and clearer than any of the others. He wanted to reach out and hold his brother and say the perfect thing. But what was the perfect thing? What could he possibly say? So Mac said nothing and watched his little brother run out of the living room past Meredith and Alice.

Nobody could have predicted that Jeremiah was about to do what he was about to do.

Mac heard the front door click open and the gusts of air whoosh in. His face dropped and he ran for the door but by the time he got there it was too late. Mac dropped to his knees at the edge of the doorframe, one hand extended into the darkness.

Jeremiah was gone.

CHAPTER 32: ALICE
Who The Hell...

The removal of me from my house happened so slowly that I almost missed it.

It started with a new chair in the living room that I never would have picked but thought looked nice enough. Then something called a snake plant, which I heard Blair tell Benny, was good for oxygenating a room. *Had the room been deoxygenated before?*

The bedroom I used to sleep in had slowly turned into a widower's bedroom. A bachelor's bedroom. It looked like an entirely different space with Benny's things tossed around it and mine gone. Or not gone, but jammed into black garbage bags and tucked away in the spare bedroom nobody ever went in.

I used to walk around the house and remember the happy moments I had shared with my family while I had been alive. In the kitchen and the living room and anywhere else. I would drift from one room to the next and let the nostalgia wash over me and comfort me and distract me from the fact of my own death. But lately it had become harder and harder for me to connect to those moments.

On one hand I felt that this was the place I belonged. I recognized this as my house. My home. Mine. But on the other hand, the more time that passed, the more bits and pieces that were changed out replaced and rearranged, the more I found it difficult to find a space for myself within it.

Thankfully, the tub had stayed the same. I climbed in and wouldn't let myself think of anything until I had taken ten full, deep breaths. I thought it would make me feel better or more levelheaded. I thought it might help me understand what had just happened or at least relax me even a tiny bit. It didn't.

I knew there must be more to the story than the angry 12-year-old side Meredith and I had heard from the door. But what could Mac possibly have on his side that would make any difference.

And where had that angry 12-year-old gone? What happened when you lunged yourself out the door into that darkness? Would Jeremiah ever come back? *Could* Jeremiah ever come back?

When it had been me hurling myself at the open door it had been a mistake. I hadn't realized that there was nothing on the other side. But Jeremiah knew. He must've known. He must have thought about it. Or maybe that was the problem, maybe he hadn't thought about it at all and then he did it and then it was too late to take it all back and he was gone.

I let my neck roll back on the edge of the tub and tried to find a second of calm but all I could hear in my mind was Jeremiah, shrieking, sobbing. *You're the reason I'm dead. You did this. You killed me. Let me go. Just let me leave this place. You're the reason I can't move on. You killed me. This is your fault. Let me go. Please!*

I wouldn't have believed Jeremiah if Mac hadn't stood there and taken it the way he did. He had the most dazed expression on his face. He didn't fight back. And as I watched I kept thinking, *fight back! Fight back! Tell him he's wrong.*

But he never did. He just took it.

I stayed in that tub for three days straight and stared out the window. It was my favourtie time of year, the end of spring, just on the edge of summer. The skies were solid blue and the sun through the window would have felt hot on my skin, might have even burned me, had I had been able to feel things like temperature. I would have happily taken the sunburn too. I would have enjoyed the process. The feeling of the heat, comforting at first, then a bit too much, then sore. I would have enjoyed the sensation of feeling something. The capability of it. Even the pain.

I watched the sun rise up in the sky and then set. Three times. I watched Benny shower in the morning and brush his teeth at night. And around the time I knew the twins would be going to bed I sang to them from my porcelain crib. It was the first time I had missed sitting between their beds for the bedtime song in months. But I couldn't risk leaving and seeing Mac. I wasn't ready.

At first I was angry that he didn't come and find me to immediately to explain himself and set it right. Then I slowly became grateful for the privacy and even afraid of being interrupted.

I wondered what was going on beyond the bathroom door. What were they doing? Were Meredith and Mac talking? Was I over-reacting? Would things ever be the same? Would things go back to normal? *Could* things go back to normal?

Three days seemed to be the amount of time I needed to let the questions subside. It was a Sunday morning and Benny had already been in to pee but he didn't bother changing out of his tee shirt and stripped pj pants. While Saturdays had always been our get things done days, Sundays had always been our take it easy and avoid getting dressed for as long as possible days.

About an hour after seeing Benny I heaved myself out of the tub and padded down the steps, looking back and forth for a sign of Meredith or Mac. But there was nobody.

I could hear the familiar giggles of both Casey and Charlie coming from the kitchen and like a magnet I was immediately drawn in to them. It had been so long since I had seen their little faces, their wispy hair, their miniature fingers. I missed them even more than I had realized and suddenly felt like an idiot for hiding out in the tub when I could have been with them.

As I walked down the hall to the kitchen the smell of blueberry pancakes floated through the air and I couldn't help but think how lucky Benny had been to catch a nanny like Blair. He really was incredible. But then I remembered that it was a Sunday and Blair didn't work on Sundays. As I came around the corner I couldn't tell if I was more surprised to find Benny at the stove, barefoot with an apron tied around his waist as he expertly flipped a pancake or Mac in the corner seemingly waiting for me. Staring at me.

I pretended not to notice Mac and focused all my attention on Benny. It was easy enough to do since I had never in my life seen him hold a spatula, let alone use one properly. I walked to the counter to survey the plate of already cooked pancakes. They almost looked better than mine. I didn't know if I should feel proud or jealous so I decided it was okay to feel a little of both.

Casey and Charlie sat at the kitchen island pouring pools of maple syrup on their empty plates every time Benny turned his back on them. Never leave the syrup unattended I thought to myself. I smiled as I realized I was happy that amongst all the loveliness and perfection that was the Sunday morning before me Benny had made such a small, rookie mistake. Something as simple as leaving the syrup unattended. I knew it wasn't a competition but I couldn't help but feel that if it had been I might've won.

Benny plopped a stack of small pancakes on each syrupy plate and the twins dug in, using both their fingers and forks to devour their breakfast. Benny was pouring them each a glass of orange juice when his phone buzzed on the counter top. It must have flashed for only a few moments but a few moments was enough for me to see the text message notification from someone called Collet.

Benny put the juice down mid-pour and picked up his phone, his face suddenly turned sheepish and then borderline giddy as he read the message and quickly replied.

I could feel Mac in the corner of the kitchen, staring at me, trying to make eye contact, or at least trying to make me acknowledge him. No, I thought. Not yet.

Instead, I focused on Benny. He put the phone down and leaned across the counter on his forearms towards the twins who were still busy wolfing down their pancakes like they might be taken away from them.

"How would you guys likes to go to the park today? This morning actually. Once we're done with breakfast."

The feasting paused and two massive smiles spread across the twins' faces. Pancakes and the park inside of one morning was beyond any kind of jackpot they could've imagined.

"Can we ride our bikes?" Casey said and shoved a forkful of fluff into his mouth.

"This park might be a little too far for that."

"What park?" Charlie said.

"A new park just on the other side of town. I don't think I've taken you there before. But I have it on good authority that it's an excellent one. Trust me."

Good authority? Whose good authority? And what was wrong with the great park just two blocks over that I could sort of but not really see from the window upstairs? Why did they need to go across town for a slide and some swings and— Of course, I thought to myself. It all made sense. This wasn't about a park. It was about someone Benny had found on that online dating thing. The coffee date woman. And now he thought he was going to take the twins to meet her at some park on the other side of town. Absolutely not, I thought to myself. I won't let this happen. Who does this woman think she is? I simply refuse to allow—

And then I remembered. I had no choice. There was not a single thing I could do about it.

***

While the twins brushed their teeth and changed out of their pajamas, I followed Benny to our bedroom, stomping more than walking, even though I knew it was a futile effort and that the only people who could actually hear me couldn't have cared less.

I sat on the edge of the tub and watched Benny get ready for the fourth day in a row. As he brushed his teeth I saw him watching his arm in the mirror and then for the first time in our marriage, actually the first time ever, I watched Benny with his toothbrush still dangling out of his mouth, lift his left arm to a 90 degree angle and flex at himself in the mirror. I would have laughed had I not been so horrified.

He finished brushing and then moved on to his hair, shifting the part from one side to the other, wetting his fingers and tousling the strands. Finally, I watched as he gurgled mouthwash, spit and looked back up at himself in the mirror with a smile. A big smile.

Who was this guy? And more importantly, who the hell was this new woman?

***

"You must know something about her? Anything? You must've at least heard of her?" I said sitting on the couch next to Meredith who had just unraveled her scarf for probably the thousandth time and was starting again.

"I'm sorry Honey, I wish I did but the name doesn't ring a bell. But you know me, I'm always the last one to know about these kinds of things."

I slumped in my seat and exhaled loudly. I wanted her to know how unhelpful the answer was to me even though I knew it wasn't really her fault and there was nothing she could do about it.

"Have you asked the others?" she said, almost innocent.

"You mean Mac? He's the only 'other' left."

"True."

"Well I can't ask Mac."

"Why not?"

"You know why."

"Okay I know why. But you gotta get over it and talk to him eventually, right?"

"What? No. I don't know if I can." I turned to face her. "Have you?"

"Of course."

"But how? I mean, how can you just forget what you heard? Doesn't it change, like, everything?"

"No."

"No?"

"Listen, I'm not here to judge anyone. Not my

job. And thank god for that. And lets not forget he just lost his brother and not that I know what happens when you jump out the door, but I think we can all agree it's nothing particularly good."

"But surely there are exceptions to these kinds of things. I mean he—"

"Not for me." I must have been gaping at her and it must have made her slightly uncomfortable because she put her knitting needles down for the first time in the conversation and turned to face me. "Look. I base my opinion of a person on how that person treats me." She paused and I knew we were both thinking of the night Mac had asked her to dance. "Period." She said and held my stare for a few more seconds before picking her needles back up and resuming clicking like nothing had happened. "Jeremiah might have had his reasons for being angry at Mac. But I don't. And from what I can tell, neither do you."

She was right. I had been spending the past few days thinking I had lost the person I had become closest to in the house, but the truth was he was still there. The person I knew was still there. Mac had seen me at my worst, seen the nastiest bits of me that I usually hid but had no choice but to display here in the afterlife. And he was still my friend.

And while I still thought there were probably expectations to every rule and I wasn't convinced everything could just go back to normal, I knew Meredith was right and the least I could do was hear him out.

Plus. I needed to know what he knew about Collet.

CHAPTER 33: MAC
Where Have You Gone?

It took some begging, but in the end Mac convinced Meredith to keep her mouth shut about Collet. He needed to be the one to tell Alice because he knew it was all he had and that without it Alice would have no reason to talk to him and would likely carry on freezing him out. Possibly forever.

I'll do this for you because I feel like I owe you one, but if I do this for you, you gotta know what's gonna happen. She's gonna have questions and you're gonna have to be ready to answer them. Are you ready for that?

When Meredith asked him, the answer had been easy, obvious even. But now that he had agreed to it and he knew it was only a matter of time before Alice came to him, he felt unsure. What if honesty was a mistake? What if it all just backfired and ended up being too much for Alice and just pushed her further away. It was precisely the reason he had avoided telling her anything sooner – to avoid exactly what had happened. He had already lost his brother and he knew he still had Meredith but he couldn't stand the idea of losing anyone else. Especially not Alice. Not yet. Not like this.

Alice found him in Benny's study, sitting at the bench looking out the window. Mac hoped it wasn't obvious but he had picked this room specifically. He wanted somewhere quiet and relatively private. It worked.

Mac heard footsteps move down the hallway and then stop at what he guessed was the door. He didn't turn around to check though. It was important that Alice make the first move here.

Seconds passed but nothing happened. Mac wanted to turn around, just to see that Alice was actually standing there. Or at least that someone was standing there. But he resisted. Instead, he tightened his grip around his thigh and waited.

He counted the seconds in his mind. Slowly. *One... two... three... four... five... six... seven...*

"I know you know I'm standing here." The words came at last and Mac let his fingers loosen. He turned to find Alice leaning against the doorframe, arms crossed. Even in her red flannel pajamas she still managed to look stern and if Mac hadn't been so nervous about the conversation he knew was coming he might have been impressed. She had come such a long way, even if she hadn't realized it yet.

"Of course I know you're standing there. But what could I possibly say?"

"I guess that's why you never came to find me? Three days and you never came—"

"I wanted to—Meredith wouldn't let me." Mac paused and ran his fingers through his hair. "She said it would be best for me to give you space. And to be honest, I wasn't doing so well after Jeremiah —I still can't believe he…"

From the corner of his eye Mac could see Alice nodding. Did that mean Alice understood?

"It's okay I get it. It was all… A lot." Alice said, her voice quiet.

"So what happens now? I mean, where do we go from here? Meredith said you would have questions so what are your questions? I'll answer them all if it means making this go away."

"I don't know if it's possible to make it all go away."

In the few seconds of silence that passed Mac stopped and started what felt like over a million different arguments, reasons why she was wrong, but his thoughts were cut off by more of her words.

"How about you just start at the beginning and we'll go from there." Alice said as she sat down on the love seat against the wall opposite Mac who remained sitting by the window. He watched her pull her legs up and tuck her toes underneath herself. She was settling in. She was ready.

It was the beginning of June 1954 and everything was ahead of Mac. In less than a month he was set to graduate high school and then after a final summer with the friends he had grown up with, he was set to pack everything he had into his newly acquired and slightly rusted but still very reliable station wagon and head off to start university seven and a half hours away.

It was going to be the first time in this life that he would be a singular person. Just Mac. Not, Mac the son of John and Judy Tullbridge. Not, Mac the older brother of the wannabe body-builder. Mac. Just Mac. And he was looking forward to it.

Just like every other 17-year-old around him, he had spent his life being defined by the people surrounding him and he was ready to be defined by himself. To really figure out what it felt like to be the person he was meant to be.

To make things even better, Mac had finally, *finally,* convinced the ultimate Liza Liz-Patrick to accompany him to the graduation dance. This was the cherry on top and as far as Mac was concerned, life couldn't have gotten better. Everything that his life would be was balancing on the horizon. He could see it, he reach for it, he could almost touch it. Almost.

The graduation dance was the reason Mac had died in that blue ruffled tux. Liza had made him rent it twice. Once for the actual day and once for practice. Today was the practice.

His parents were out for the afternoon doing

errands and he was officially on babysitting duty, but how much babysitting could a 12 year old take?

Mac walked down the stairs, adjusting his shirtsleeves under the jacket as the doorbell rang. Liza had arrived. He sprang down the rest of the stairs, jumping the final four, his new brogues landing on the hardwood with a crack.

The commotion drew Jeremiah from his bedroom upstairs. He was halfway down the steps and only barely visible from the front door when Mac opened the door and Liza Liz-Patrick, dressed in matching blue lace and tulle and tights appeared. Mac was mesmerized. Of course he was.

"You look great, Doll." Mac said and from the stairs he heard a small snicker. Mac whipped his head around to find Jeremiah perched on a step in the middle of the stairs watching.

"What are you looking at you little perv?"

"Just a couple of clowns." Jeremiah muttered, purposely loud enough for everyone to hear. Liza gasped.

Mac's face clouded over with an expression Jeremiah clearly recognized because the mischievous grin immediately dropped from Jeremiah's face. Mac puffed up his chest and in two giant leaps he had Jeremiah under his arm, his nose pressing into his armpit.

"What did you say you little perv? You wanna say that again, I didn't hear you the first time."

It was more of a show than Mac was used to putting on but Liza Liz-Patrick was watching after all. She deserved a show. She demanded one.

Jeremiah managed to twist his way out of Mac's grip and scamper up a few steps, putting distance between himself and his peacocking brother.

"Jeez take it easy, Mac. I was only joking."

"You're the joke, Jeremiah." Mac spat out. He was on a roll and though he knew he was being harsh he felt that he couldn't stop himself now. He didn't want to. "You think you can make fun of what we're wearing? Take a look a yourself buddy. What, I supposed you're going to "workout"? That your workout gear? You wouldn't know a workout if it slapped you in the face." Mac faked a quick slap across Jeremiah's face and it worked beautifully, better than he could have planned. Jeremiah flinched backward, missed a step and tripped, hitting his head on the wall as he fell. Mac laughed and pointed as Jeremiah quickly picked himself up. Mac felt no pity, adrenaline pumped through him.

"You think you're so big and strong, huh? Well I've got news for you. I used your little weight set this morning. Easiest thing I've ever done."

"You touched my weights!?"

"You bet I did."

"You're not allowed to touch them. They're mine! I'm going to tell mom and dad!"

"See if I care."

"But you don't even lift weights." Jeremiah said and almost immediately a snicker came from behind Mac. From Liza Liz-Patrick.

"You bet your scrawny butt I do. In fact. I need heavier ones. The ones you got down there are for babies."

"No way. Did you try the full bar set?"

Mac nodded though Jeremiah was right, he'd never touched a weight in his life and actually didn't even know what a full bar set meant. "Hardly felt a thing." He said, tasting the lie on his lips and liking it.

"I don't believe you."

"And what makes you think I care even the tiniest bit what you believe?"

Mac watched as Jeremiah's face scrunched up. Was he going to cry? *Oh please let him cry.*

But Jeremiah didn't cry. Mac watched his little brother stare at him. Silent. Assessing him. Judging him. It unnerved him. Mac realized Jeremiah was taking him in and not liking what he found. In a small corner of himself Mac knew he had gone too far. It was out of character and as usual it had come on so quickly he hadn't realized what was happening until it was too late to stop. And even then he didn't know why but he didn't stop.

Jeremiah grunted, turned and sulked up the rest of the stairs, rubbing his head and looking over his shoulder as he moved.

"Yeah." Mac said in reply to Jeremiah's silence. "And you better stay out of our way." Mac said. "I'm in charge till mom and dad get home."

The slam of Jeremiah's bedroom door was the only response and for a second shame prickled at Mac. But just for a second. Then he turned back to Liza Liz-Patrick.

"So is that your car out there?"

"Sure is." Mac said with more pride than the car was worth. "Wanna check her out?"

"You bet!" She purred and giggled.

Mac patted his pocket and smiled. Like every other freshly minted teenage driver, Mac was never without his car keys.

They hurried out the front door and Mac smiled as he opened the passenger door for Liza. Practice for the big day. She smiled and giggled and as they climbed onto the station wagon bench seat the vinyl cracked and squeaked.

"Pretty cool, huh?" Mac said as he flicked an invisible speck of dust off the wheel and grinned.

"Well aren't you going to start it up?" Liza said. "Take me out for a spin."

The look on her face told Mac she knew he wasn't allowed to leave Jeremiah alone. That putting the keys in the ignition would be breaking the rules. The look on her face was a dare.

When Mac didn't move, Liza smirked and something about the expression on her face told Mac she thought he wouldn't do it. Too scared or something. He started the car.

Really, he thought to himself, what trouble could possibly come from one quick whip around the block?

Mac was gone for exactly twelve minutes and forty-five seconds with approximately nine and a half of those minutes spent driving and the remaining three minutes and fifteen seconds spent trying to build up the courage to kiss Liza Liz-Patrick. They sat in the car parked at the curb in front of her house and she waited, but nothing happened. Next time, Mac told himself. *Definitely* next time.

As Mac pulled into the driveway he felt unexpectedly relieved. Everything looked exactly the same as he had left it, nothing was on fire. Everything seemed fine.

Mac knew Jeremiah would be crabby with him, and he knew he probably deserved it. He wasn't even sure where half the things he said had come from, but he was confident he could make up for it now. After all, what couldn't a drive in his big brother's car to get an ice cream fix?

"Jer!" Mac called as he sprang through the front door, one hand still on the handle. He was ready to go now but there was no reply. *Okay, playing hard to get are ya?* Mac left the door open and skipped up the steps, taking two at a time. "Jer?" He said as he knocked on Jeremiah's bedroom door. He paused to listen. Still nothing. He carefully opened the door, slowly at first, until it became obvious that the room as empty. Mac frowned. *Where have you gone?*

Then he remembered Jeremiah had been in his workout clothes. That grey sweatshirt, the red gym shorts, his tennis shoes.

Mac turned on his heel, slipping slightly from the slickness of the new soles and made his way back down the stairs. He opened the door to the basement and called out again. "Jer! Finish up! I'm taking you for ice cream!"

Silence.

"Jer!"

Silence.

"Oh come on, Jer." Mac said and thudded down the stairs. "Why do you always have to be so dramatic—"

Silence.

CHAPTER 34: ALICE
You Have Me Too

"This used to be his bedroom, you know. I was always a little bit jealous because he got the room with the good window."

I stared at him and waited for him to finish the story.

"Good people-watching from up here. You used to be able to see all the way to—"

"Finish the story, Mac." I said.

"What more is there to say?" He said and stared at me.

"What happened when you went downstairs?" I said, only about half convinced I wanted him to tell me.

"He was dead." Mac's voice was plain and he looked at me when I didn't say anything. "You want the dirty details? Okay. When I went downstairs I found my little brother lying on his bench with a weighted bar crushed against his throat. And do you know what was on that bar? Those weights I said I could lift but had actually never touched in my life."

Mac dropped his head and ran his fingers

through his hair.

"I called an ambulance but it was too late. The bar had flattened his trachea and he suffocated before he could get himself out from under it." Mac paused and looked out the window. "My parents came home as they we loading his body onto the gurney. I knew I wouldn't be able to stop my Father, but I thought I could at least save my Mother from seeing it. I had such a tight grip around her but she still managed to break free. I had no idea she was so strong."

I walked over to Mac and sat next to him on the window bench but he wouldn't look at me. "It wasn't your fault Mac. Not really. It was an accident."

"That's what my parents told me. I tired to believe them, but I could tell that they didn't even believe it themselves."

So many of the little questions I had about Mac and Jeremiah suddenly found an answer. And though I had tried to figure it out before, I never could have predicted this. It all made so much sense. The tension between the brothers, the resentment, the guilt, the anger. Even the red bruise across Jeremiah's throat, which I had clearly misinterpreted.

Everything made sense and lined up except for one thing and I didn't know how to ask.

"So if... but then how... how did... " I fidgeted

with the edge of my pyjama shirt. "I mean, you're wearing the tux...so—"

"How did I die?"

"Well, yeah." I said, suddenly sheepish. Like maybe I'd been a touch too nosey, asked one too many questions, pushed just a little bit too far.

"Let me ask you something."

"Okay."

"Could you live with yourself if you knew you'd done what I'd done?"

"Mac, it wasn't your fault—"

"Just answer the question, Alice. Had you been in my shoes, would you have been able to live with yourself?"

And then I realized what he was saying.

"Everyone went to bed early that night. Or at least that's what we told each other but I doubt anyone actually slept. My first choice would have been my Dad's Colt .22 but he kept it in a drawer in his bedside table. I couldn't' wait that long." Mac paused and I waited for him to continue. No more pushing from me.

"And that was all she wrote." Mac said and clapped his hands once. "Next thing I knew it was morning. I was sitting in my car in the garage, windows down, and Jeremiah was standing directly in front of the car. His arms were crossed and he was staring at me. Just waiting for me to wake up or something. And as soon as he saw me open my eyes, I still remember it so clearly, he just shook his head and walked away. Not a single word. And I had no idea what was going on. I thought it had all been a bad dream or something. I thought my dead brother was actually alive. It didn't occur to me that actually we were both dead."

"Even though you did it yourself?"

"Yeah you'd think that would help, wouldn't you? But it was all just an empty memory to me. Anyway, I obviously ran after Jeremiah into the house and that was when I found this guy in a suit that turned out to be Dr. Peter Cassidy. Big surprise, he didn't say much. Just that I was dead. That I had killed myself and that it seemed we were all trapped in some kind of afterlife. He called it the middle ground."

"So when your parents woke up the next morning they found out they had not one, but two dead sons?"

Mac's head snapped away from the window for the first time during the conversation. His eyes locked directly onto mine. "Don't judge me for something you could never understand."

"I'm not judging you." I said.

Mac continued to stare and I could see his face softening, his jaw easing, his tight, squinting eyes loosening up. Roo shifted for the first time since the conversation had started. He put his head in Mac's lap and licked his thumb once.

"That's not a bad name for it, actually." I said.

"What?"

"Middle ground. It makes sense. A place between places, you know. That's what it was for the doc and for Jeremiah and I'm guessing it is for all of us. Once we do whatever the hell it is we need to do here."

"It might be for you guys. But not for me."

"What do you mean, of course it's the same for you."

"Have you ever wondered why a dog would be here?"

"What?" I said, thrown by the change of topic.

Mac patted Roo's head. "Why's he here? It doesn't make sense. What kind of unfinished business could a dog possibly have?"

I shrugged my shoulders. I had no idea. I'd never thought of it before though now that Mac brought it up, it was a good point. What *was* a dog doing in the middle ground?

"Sometimes I think his unfinished business might be me." Mac looked at me. "I know it sounds strange, selfish even, but maybe he's just here to keep me company because I'm not going anywhere. I'm here for good, ya know. No getting out of here for me, but maybe it'll be okay with my pal here."

"Mac you'll figure out what you need to do and you'll do it and you'll move on to whatever comes next."

"I already know what I need to do. But I won't do it. I can't. I'll never forgive myself for what I let happen." His face was calm and I could tell he believed what he was saying. "But hey, I'll be okay. I've got my pal here and people will always be dying so I'll always have my job welcoming folks in." He cracked a smile, trying to lighten the mood with his joke, but he must have seen my face drop and then realized what he had said. "I mean, not for a long, long time will anyone die in this house. A looong time. Oodles of time."

I smiled. I knew what he meant.

"Plus, I have Meredith. I don't think she's going anywhere fast."

"Stand up." I said. Mac looked confused but did what I asked, sliding Roo's head from his lap. Then I reached out and hugged him. Meredith was right. It wasn't our place to judge Mac for anything that had already happened. All we had was what we had right then.

"And me." I said. "You have me, too."

I could almost hear Mac smiling over my shoulder and I squeezed him a little tighter. I knew it meant something to him to hear me say that. And I meant what I said. He did have me.

CHAPTER 35: MEREDITH
A Happy Family Again

Meredith looked at the ceiling of the living room and wondered how long they were going to stay up there for. Since Alice had gone upstairs there had been hardly a sound. And the rest of the house was quiet too. Benny and the twins had been gone all day and still hadn't returned. And without the doctor or Jeremiah around, Meredith had nothing to distract herself with except her knitting. They even had the dog up there for crying out loud!

She tried to focus on the stiches, one and then another and then the next one. But it was hard. She was bored.

Meredith tossed her needles and yarn to the opposite side of the couch and as if in response to her protest, she heard footsteps upstairs. *Finally.* The steps moved along the hallway and then pattered down the steps, quickly followed by prancing paws. Meredith quickly collected her needles and straightened out the yarn. She cared about what happened up there, that they smoothed things over. But she didn't need them knowing that. If they knew she cared she'd be showing her cards and she wasn't prepared to do that.

Mac poked his head around the edge of the

door and rapped his fist on the wall.

"Knock, knock." he said. "Mind if we join?"

"Oh hi." Meredith said, pretending to be busy. "Sure, yeah, come on in."

Mac walked in with Alice following behind him and Roo following behind Alice.

"So." Meredith said. "Are we all one big happy family again?"

"Well I don't know about big." Mac said as he dropped into the chair next to the couch. "We're dropping like flies around here. Been a productive year for us." Mac heard his own words and his face clouded over, clearly thinking of Jeremiah.

"But yes." Alice said. "We are a happy family again."

"Good." Meredith said as if Mac and Alice were siblings and Meredith was the mother, pleased that her children had worked out their sibling squabble.

Meredith watched Mac and Alice who both seemed sunken into their seats, happy, small smiles of relaxation pulling on their lips. Things had felt so tense lately that the present ease was much needed.

And then Alice jerked up, her back straight, her brows pushed together. The tension was back.

"Wait." she said. "Why is it so quiet? Where

is everyone?" Meredith wondered how long it would take Alice to notice. Both Meredith and Mac looked at each other and then watched Alice stand and look out the window. "The sun is setting."

"They went out this morning. Remember?" Mac said, easing in to it. "The park." Alice's face was blank. Zero recognition. "The park they needed to drive to... On the other side of town."

"Oh." Alice's face dropped and she slowly sat back down on the couch. "Right." She looked at her wrist, apparently expecting to find a watch she had never been wearing. "But what time is it? I mean, when did they leave? That must've been hours ago?" She said, absently massaging her wrist.

"After breakfast." Meredith said and waited for Alice to burst into a flurry of rambling questions and anger. Something along the lines of: *Where were they and who were they with and it was a Sunday and there was school tomorrow and how could Benny and whoever he was with be so irresponsible?*

But there was nothing. Alice said nothing. And though Meredith was no longer alone, the room was silent again.

CHAPTER 36: ALICE
Aging Was A Privilege

By the time Benny and the kids came home the sun had been set for over two hours. And when I finally heard the key in the door I rushed to watch them come through. Benny moved slowly, with Casey draped over one of his shoulders and a sleepy-eyed Charlie holding his hand and following him through the door.

All three of them had slight sunburns on their noses, the edges of their ears and the backs of their necks. Apparently it had been a nice day.

I waited for Benny to put the kids to bed. He didn't wake Casey up to get changed and he didn't make either of them brush their teeth. When the door clicked shut I reached my hand out to Charlie's sleeping face, I wanted to touch it, feel the heat of the burn on my skin and take the burn away from him. I hovered my hand close to the skin but couldn't bring myself to touch him. I didn't want to associate touching my children with how it now felt. I preferred to hang on to the memory of how it used to feel instead of trying to turn what I had now into something that it wasn't.

I took my time singing that night. Pausing between verses, even repeating some to make the song a little long, just because I wanted to and who was going to tell me that I wasn't allowed to. I would do what I wanted to do while I still could.

When I rejoined Mac and Meredith downstairs Benny was in the living room with them and had just turned the TV on. As it came to life Benny quickly turned the volume down to an almost whisper and glanced up in the direction of the twins' bedroom. I smiled. It was sweet for him to worry but I knew how deeply asleep they were. Nothing would wake them now.

I watched him as he flicked through the channels. He had the remote in one hand and in the other was a beer, fresh from the fridge, the glass foggy and damp.

"I hope he picks something good." Mac said, from his chair. His eyes narrowed in on the screen.

"Me too." Meredith said. "Had enough of those cartoons."

"And turn it up Benny ol' pal." Mac said.

Benny's phone rang from the kitchen and at the sound he looked over his shoulder. A smile spread across his face and he dropped the remote on the couch as he hurried to catch the call before losing it to his voicemail.

"Oh look!" Meredith said. "Opening credits. It's only just starting now!"

"I wonder who's calling him? I mean, kinda late, no?" I said and we all looked at the clock on the wall. It was only 9:30. Nobody said anything.

"What's *Sleepless in Seattle*?" Mac said, reading the movie title from the screen.

"It's good." I said, only half involved in the conversation.

"What's it about?" Meredith asked.

"Two people who unexpectedly fall in love."

"Oh it's a chick film." Mac pursed his lips and half slumped in his chair but kept his eyes on the screen.

I looked over my shoulder. "Long call, no?" I said but nobody answered me. I could hear Benny laughing from the kitchen. I knew I could have gotten up, gone to the kitchen and eavesdropped as much as I wanted to and that neither Mac nor Meredith would've stopped me. They were too invested in the movie and too uninterested in what I was doing to stop me. But for some reason I stayed sitting on the couch. There was a part of me that wanted to hear that conversation. To know that it was just Blair or Charlotte or some other known and friendly figure on the other end of the line. But there was a bigger part of me that didn't want to know. Or that probably did know but didn't want to have it all confirmed. For now it was just a maybe and just a maybe was a hell of a lot more comfortable than the alternative.

Benny's voice got slightly louder and I thought

he might be coming back to the living room, but then I heard his feet on the steps and his voice slowly recede as he climbed higher and higher up the stairs.

"Jackpot!" Mac said, his arms thrown in the air.

"What?" I said.

"Ten bucks says he forgets about the TV and leave it on all night. It's so quiet he'll just go to bed without realizing."

"You don't have ten bucks."

"It's a figure of speech."

"No, it's not. It's a literal bet." I said.

"Well whatever." Mac said still grinning. "Let's just hope some good stuff comes on."

"And that it gets louder. I can hardly hear a thing." Meredith said. She was leaning forward, straining her neck closer and tilting her head to the side.

"Why don't you just move closer?" I said.

"But we can't move the furniture." Meredith said.

"So." I said.

"So we're just supposed to sit on the floor?"

"Well... Yeah."

Meredith looked at me and by the expression on her face I almost thought I had said the words in another language. But I didn't speak any other languages. She looked at the floor, then back at me and I could tell that it had clearly never occurred to her to sit on the floor.

"Why not?" I said.

"Well because... Well I don't know."

"Come sit with me." I said. "You too." I pointed at Mac.

We settled down, crossed-legged in row about two feet from the screen.

"I haven't sat on the floor in... I don't even know how long."

"That's because you're old." Mac said.

"Gee, thanks." Meredith said. And I lightly punched Mac in the shoulder.

"Well you're not anymore."

"Hey, don't take that from me. What if I like being *old?*" Meredith's voice sounded surprisingly hurt. "Aging is a privilege. I'm happy to be *old*. Especially now that I don't have the inconveniences of being old like not being able to sit on the floor."

"Okay, fine." Mac said. "You can be old."

"Thank you."

With Meredith's argument won we all turned our attention back to the movie. And while Tom Hanks and Meg Ryan fell in love I thought of Meredith's words. It was true. Aging was a privilege and

I wished I had seen it that way when I had been alive.

In the end Mac had been right and if money was a thing in the middle ground I would have owed him a tenner because the TV stayed on all night. It turned out to be a Norah Ephron marathon with Sleepless in Seattle turning into Silkwood and then When Harry Met Sally and then You've Got Mail. We were about 20 minutes into Heartburn when Blair arrived bright and early and turned the TV off. We stood from the same positions we had taken hours earlier, having enjoyed ourselves but also grateful for the reprieve.

CHAPTER 37: ALICE
A Broken Heart

The twins had been off school on summer holidays for about a month when I heard the word for the first time. *Girlfriend.* It sounded so juvenile and young and strange. Especially in relation to Benny.

I had been his girlfriend once upon a time, but I had been his wife for so much longer than that and surely that cancelled out all girlfriends, past and present. We were all adults and knew exactly what was going on. Couldn't she just be "Benny's friend"?

"Are you going to invite your *girlfriend* to the party?" Blair had said to Benny in the kitchen one morning while washing the breakfast dishes.

Benny seemed to wince at the word and I knew he must have had issues with the way it sounded too, but for some reason he didn't challenge it.

"I'm not sure. I'm wondering if it's too soon, you know? Might be weird?"

Yes! Yes it would be very weird I thought to myself even though I had no idea what party they were talking about. It didn't matter.

"No." Blair said. "The opposite I think. Collette is a fantastic woman and I think she'd really love to come."

I felt my jaw involuntarily clench and tried to remember a time when I had liked Blair. I knew there had been a time, but somehow his unrelenting support for this *girlfriend* made all my positive thoughts about him disappear.

"I'll think about it" Benny said before swallowing the last of his coffee and pulling his briefcase off the counter. "Thanks for this." Benny said and set his coffee mug down. "See you later."

"Have a good day at work." Blair said.

"You too." Benny looked over his shoulder and smiled when he said it.

With Benny out of the kitchen I walked over to Blair and stood as close to him as I could without touching him. His hands were underwater, scrubbing some dish, so I was confident he wouldn't be stepping away from the sink anytime soon. I watched him. Who did he think he was? Who asked for his opinion on anything? First with the online dating and then with this *girlfriend* business.

"What cha doing there, Alice?" I jumped at the voice and turned to find Mac standing across the kitchen watching me watch Blair. He didn't bother hiding his amusement and I didn't bother hiding my irritation at the interruption.

"What? I'm not allowed to look at him?"

"Oh so that's what you're doing?" Mac said and laughed.

"Well it's just—" I could hear my voice getting higher, defensive, I carried on anyway. "It's just how much do we really know about this guy, you know. I mean all I'm saying is how do we really know we can trust him."

"And studying his pores is going to give you that information?"

"Oh shut up."

"Blair's been here for almost a year. He's great and you're being ridiculous and I think you know that." Mac crossed his arms and smiled, smug.

"Okay whatever." I rolled my eyes. "I just don't understand why everyone is so obsessed with this Collette lady."

"You're the one who sounds obsessed with her."

"What—I'm just trying to make sure my family gets what's best for them."

"And a woman who everyone raves about just isn't good enough, is that right?"

"Why can't anyone be on my side with this?" I said and blew past Mac. Meredith. I thought. Meredith will understand. Meredith will be on my team.

I found her in the living room watching the

twins build a tower out of Jenga blocks. As I walked in the room the tower toppled and the twins laughed furiously and rushed to collect the pieces and begin again.

"Amateurs." I heard Meredith mumble before she saw me and perked up. "Oh hi, Honey."

"What do you know about this Collette woman? What do you think of her?" I dropped onto the couch next to her.

"From what I've heard she sounds like a lovely woman."

"Of for Christ's sake—" I said and tossed my arms up in the air. I didn't need to look at Mac who stood behind me to know that he was smiling. I could hear it. I could feel it. The jerk.

Out of the corner of my eye I watched him sit on the floor next to Roo who immediately put his head in Mac's lap. I wondered if being scratched and pet still felt good for him in the middle ground or if it was just about the attention. Or maybe just a force of habit.

"I just want to know what she looks like, you know. It's something people of my generation do, okay. We don't know who you are so we type your name into a little box on the computer and don't stop until we've memorized every scrap of information it can spit out.

"What kind of stuff can it find?" Mac asked.

"Anything. Everything." I said. "Social media accounts first. But then there's other stuff like anything that's been written in the newspaper or published online. It's a vortex. And I want to throw this Collet woman into the vortex and see what it digs up."

"What about privacy?" Mac asked. I wanted to be empathetic. The concept of the Internet and social media and Google was probably incomprehensible to him. But his questions felt like more of him taking her side instead of mine so I ignored him. I didn't care about her privacy and didn't want him to care about it either.

"And what does it matter what she looks like anyway?" Mac said.

"It *always* matters what the other woman looks like." Meredith said, finally injecting herself into the conversation in a useful way.

"Well she was at the funeral. You probably saw her there."

"My funeral?"

"That's the one."

I scanned my memories of the day but couldn't remember seeing a fantastic, lovely, utterly remarkable woman like the one everyone described. "Well I don't remember her." I said, dismissing the thought.

"Sounds like a *you* kind of problem then." Mac

said, smiling again. Why was he enjoying this?

"Listen, excuse me for not remembering every person who set foot in this house that day. I'll admit I might have been slightly distracted by the fact that I was *dead*."

"Easy." Mac said and held his hands up. "I get it." And though I knew he was done he still had that smile on his face and all I wanted to do was reach over and smack it right off. But I knew he wouldn't feel it and it would probably only provoke him.

I flopped back onto the couch and watched Casey slowly add another block to the top of the Jenga tower. She was so careful. So precise. The last time I had played Jenga with her she had been so terrible I almost felt bad playing with her. Like it might hurt her self-esteem or something. But clearly things had changed. She had grown so much.

And Charlie had grown too, in different ways. He was still just as reckless with the Jenga pieces as he had always been, but he was more patient with Casey, kinder, more aware of the fact that others existed in the same world as him. It wasn't that he had been particularly self-centered before; it was that all children were self-involved until they weren't. Or until it at least faded a bit. And it was fading for Charlie. Where before he would have knocked the tower over if Casey took too long on her turn, he now sat and watched and waited. I was proud of him.

"Hey Meredith?" I said "How did you die?" The words came from out of nowhere and fell from my mouth quickly and casually. As if I was were asking her what her middle name was or her favourtie colour.

"Alice?" Mac said, bringing some sense of social protocol to the conversation.

"I'm sorry it's just that I just realized I don't know and I thought we knew pretty much everything about each other. Or at least the big stuff."

"Broken heart." Meredith said, equally as casually as when I had asked. Her eyes still fixed on her knitting needles.

Mac snorted and I glared at him. This time I was the one reminding him of social protocol.

"I'm sorry." Mac said. "But a broken heart isn't a cause of death. A condition, maybe. But you can't die from it."

"I did."

"I was here Meredith, remember? I saw you die. You just… drifted off in your sleep or something. Old age."

"Says who?"

Mac gawked. "I don't know. Like… everyone."

"No. Not everyone. Not me."

"Fine." Mac said. "Please, tell us. What does it feel like to die of a broken heart." I think he meant his words to sound sarcastic but when he heard them out loud his face dropped and I could tell he regretted it and hoped she wouldn't answer.

Of course, Meredith rose to occasion and put Mac squarely in his place.

"Well, first it's the most disorienting thing you've ever felt. You don't know what's happened. Or how it could have happened. There's no logic. You keep waiting to wake up but you never do. And you don't sleep either so there's no reprieve. And then there's the worry. Are they okay, wherever they are? Will I be okay? What will happen now? What will I do? How will I live? And then it becomes physical. All you do is cry and when you've cried so much that your body is so thoroughly dehydrated that it physically can't produce tears anymore you just heave and choke and you try to breath but air doesn't feel the way it used to. It doesn't feed you or energize you or soothe you anymore. Nothing does and you know nothing ever will. You stop showering. You forget about food.

And then finally, you put yourself to bed, not to sleep, but to die because you know you won't wake up. And you let that thing that's been pushing down on you finally push the final bit until there's nothing left for it to push down on because you're dead. And you've died of a broken heart."

I sat wide-eyed watching Meredith watch Mac. Her eyes challenged him to tell her she was wrong and that she hadn't died of a broken heart. Mac, thankfully, stayed silent.

"And when I went to bed that night all I could think was please let him be there, please let him be there, please let him be there. But he wasn't there. I didn't know what or where "there" was, but if I was going somewhere I wanted him to be there too. But he wasn't. And as you say, you were there. You know exactly what I woke up to – a big smile and a face full of blue ruffles." Meredith looked to me. "Friggen terrifying." She said and looked back at Mac who nodded and I realized he hadn't been joking when he told me months ago that his first time welcoming someone into the middle ground hadn't gone so well.

"Any questions?" Meredith said, perky and polite.

Mac bit his lips together and shook his head no, his eyes almost as wide as mine.

"And you." She said turning to me, the same stern tone still ringing through her voice. I gaped. *What had I done? Why was I now in line of fire? Go back to Mac!* I silently pleaded. "No woman." She continued, her finger shaking and pointing at me. "No matter how fantastic or lovely or whatever else you've heard, will be ever be able to replace you. Got it?"

I nodded and could feel my eyes still bulging, my lips pressed together. I wasn't about to contradict her. Nobody in their right mind would.

"Good." Meredith said and picked up her knitting again. "I'm making a sweater this time." She nodded to the project in her lap. "And the damn collar gives me hell every time."

I looked over to Mac who stared back at me, mirroring my shock.

The Jenga tower toppled once again and the room erupted in seven-year-old laughter.

CHAPTER 38: MAC
A Casual Saturday BBQ

Mac had been skeptical of the event that had been unofficially been dubbed "the party" since the first time he heard about it. And when he had asked Alice what she thought it was for she had been flippant and told him it was just a summer BBQ with a handful of friends. She said it was something they used to do every summer. She said it wasn't a big deal.

"In the summer, people throw BBQs for no reason."

"But what's this one for?"

"For the sake of summer!" Alice said. "That's what people do!"

"But it just seems like everyone is make a big deal of this. There must be a reason."

"Fine. If you need a reason the reason is that it's summer and the sun is out and it's a nice thing to do on a Saturday. Why is that so strange to you? Didn't you ever do that?"

"I guess." Mac said, still unconvinced. He didn't want to say too much in case he was wrong. But he was *so* sure he was right. Mac prided himself on his observation skills and he was sure that he had this one pegged. Too many things were lining up too perfectly for him to be wrong.

And on the day of the party itself, even more things fell into place. The first thing was Charlotte. She came bursting through the front door just after 10am pulling Dale behind her who pulled three suitcases behind him. The twins were thrilled at the sight of their 'fun' Auntie and Alice became preoccupied with watching them and the smiles on their faces.

Mac watched too, but for different reasons. What was Charlotte doing at the house? Florida was a long way to come for a casual Saturday BBQ, wasn't it?

The next thing was the groceries. By noon the kitchen was dotted with huge bags of supplies. Everything for the grill, buns, condiments, beer, wine, ice. Everything needed for a casual BBQ but multiplied by about 20.

"Seem like a lot of food." Mac said to Alice, trying to get her to see it. But she brushed him off.

"I always did the shopping. Benny probably had no idea how much to buy and thought better safe than sorry."

The third thing was Alice's parents. They arrived just before 4pm along with Blair and his husband just as Benny was firing up the grill. That was when Mac thought Alice might realize something was going on. But if she did, she didn't say anything.

By 6pm the party was humming along, but because most of the guests were in the backyard the house was mostly empty, leaving plenty of room for the three of them to watch from the kitchen windows which were conveniently wide open. Occasionally someone would come in to find more potato salad or extra ketchup, but for the most part they had the place to themselves.

It was the kind of party Mac knew Jeremiah would have loved. Lots of action but also lots of space for observation. And plus, Charlotte was there. He felt a quick pang of sadness as he remembered how for reasons he had never been able to pin down, Jeremiah had always been so drawn to her.

Mac wanted to talk to Meredith and Alice about Jeremiah but it all felt too soon. The kid had thrown himself out the door into literal nothingness just to finally get away from him. On the one hand Mac wondered if Jeremiah had finally found some peace, but on the other he doubted that peace could be found in the place Jeremiah had so willingly leapt.

Mac knew he would talk about it eventually, but for now at least he was still processing and without even a word on it, Meredith and Alice seemed to understand. He would bring it up when he was ready. After all, he told himself, he had nothing but time.

Middle Ground

Mac looked back out the window at the crowd of people and traced Alice's stare. It was clear what was stopping Alice from seeing everything else around her. Not a what, actually, but a who. Collette. She had arrived with her son just before Alice's parents and since then Alice's attention had been focused only on her.

By the time Benny stood on a chair and tapped his giant BBQ flipper against his beer Mac knew he had been right all along. There was definitely a reason the party.

CHAPTER 39: ALICE
Someplace New

My first impression of Collet was that she looked very normal. Now that she was in front of me I realized that I did recognize her from the funeral and maybe even the twins' 7th birthday party, but only vaguely. I think I accused her of being his therapist or something. She looked like a therapist. She wore blowy linen clothes and hardly any make up. And she was definitely older than me, which surprised me. Up until that moment I had thought it almost mandatory that a man's second wife be at least 10 years younger than his first.

It turned out that she wasn't a therapist. She was a professor in a different department but at the same university as Benny. Or so I heard her say to Charlotte who luckily stood interrogating the woman only a few feet from the window.

I realized Charlotte was treating Collette exactly the same way she had always treated me and wondered if Charlotte's bite hadn't necessarily been about me but about any woman Benny dated.

I almost felt bad for the woman, but she knew how to hold her own and even up against Charlotte's pressure, Collet's voice was smooth and clam. She was intelligent and articulate but also gentle. And I couldn't help but smile when she managed to out-wit Charlotte's playful banter not once, but twice. I caught myself thinking these things, these adjectives and stopped short, almost physically recoiling from the window. Did I... *like her?* Or if like was too much, did I at least not hate her? I could feel Mac watching me and didn't care enough to tell him to go away. I wasn't doing anything wrong. I wasn't whining or complaining. I was just watching. I squinted and kept staring at her, daring her ugly side to show itself.

That was when I heard Benny clang his metal spatula against his beer bottle. He looked ridiculous standing on that chair trying to get everyone's attention but it worked. Everyone stopped talking and turned their attention to him. Even me.

"Hi everybody." He said and a few beer soaked folks cheered him on. His voice was unsteady and nervous. "I wanted to thank everyone for coming. It means more to me and to the kids than I would ever know how to say." He paused and the crowd was silent. This was exactly the moment I would have stepped in and helped wrap up the speech but from my window there was nothing I could do so just like everyone else, I watched and waited. *Say something. Say something quick Benny, it's getting weird!*

"Alice is the only woman who could ever

make me do this."

"What?" I said.

"I knew it." Mac whispered, clapped and turned in a quick spin of dance movement.

"What's going on?" I said and looked at Mac and then at Meredith for an answer. They both shook their heads and with one gentle finger Meredith steered my face back to the window.

"Alice was an incredible wife. A phenomenal mother." Benny's eyes were wet and his voice slightly choked. He looked out at the crowd who mirrored his expression. He cleared his throat and continued.

"I don't want today to be a sad day. I purposely chose a memorial like this because I know it's exactly what she would have wanted."

"A memorial?"

"Alice loved the summer and being outside and having her friends and family around. She would've loved today and I'm not about to claim I know what happens when we leave this place, but I hope in some way she's here with us today."

I'm here! I'm right here!

"Alice was like no other woman I've ever know. She didn't care about things. She cared about people. And the world would be a better place if more people cared about other people the way she did. Having lost her so soon, so young, is a tragedy. But it is the greatest blessing I've ever had to have shared my life with her, even for the small amount of time I was able to."

Benny paused but this time it wasn't awkward, it was necessary. He looked down to collect himself and when he looked back up his eyes were red but his smile was whole and real. He held up his beer and the crowd followed, each guest offering up their glass in his direction.

"To Alice." He said. "Wherever you are, you are loved and so deeply missed."

"To Alice." The crowd replied in humming unison.

I felt Mac and Meredith on either of my sides, holding me, though nobody said a word. I watched Benny step down from his stage and guests mill about, dabbing their eyes, smiling, hugging. I had been so preoccupied with Collette that I hadn't even noticed my parents, or colleagues from the school I had taught at, or the friends I went to school with myself. They were all there, right in front of me.

"I need a minute." I said and wiggled my way out of Mac and Meredith's hug.

"Alice, don't go." Mac said.

"No, I'm fine, really. Just need a minute. I'll be back soon." I said and hurried out of the kitchen.

"Let her go." I heard Meredith tell Mac and I

knew he wouldn't follow.

When I said I only needed a minute I really did think that was all the time I needed and had planned on rejoining them at the window. But instead, I spent the rest of the party watching alone from the twin's bedroom window. It had become a place that was even more comforting to me than the bathtub.

I think somewhere deep inside of me I knew why I decided to stay upstairs. I think I knew it was going to happen before it did and I wondered if it had been the same for Dr. Peter Cassidy. Did something in him shift the way I had felt something shift so clearly inside of me?

It all seemed so clear to me. I didn't need to be 'somebody' in order to be somebody worth remembering. I didn't need to be extraordinary to be loved. I didn't need to be more than everything that I was in order to be worthy of being missed and grieved for. I was enough and for the first time in my life, and death for that matter, I believed it more than anything.

I knew I didn't have long and that there were things I wanted to do and say and see before whatever came next came for me. I wanted to see Benny's face one last time and watch my beautiful twins playing and smiling and laughing just once more. I wanted to tell Meredith that I valued her friendship and that I believed her when she said she had died of a broken heart and I wanted her to believe me when I told her that if I could fix it for her, I would.

But more than anything I wanted to tell Mac that he was like a brother I never had and that I loved him and that even if he couldn't forgive himself he needed to know and believe that everyone else did, even Jeremiah. Wherever he was.

I was just about to stand when it happened. A warmth that started in my toes and slowly, gently moved up my body. It felt like liquid sunshine moving through me, warming me when I hadn't realized I'd been cold. It heated my belly and my heart. I felt it reach out to my fingers then up my neck and down each and every strand of my hair.

In so many ways I wasn't ready to go, I wanted to stay for just a little bit longer. But the warmth was too welcome.

I let my head rest against the windowsill and allowed it to take over me as I listened to the soundtrack of my loved ones remembering me. And as my children laughed and my friends and family chatted below, I found peace and drifted off to someplace new.

Made in the USA
San Bernardino, CA
14 March 2020